THE FIVE ANCESTORS

龍 Dragon

Jeff Stone

The Five Ancestors

THE FIVE ANCESTORS

龍 Dragon
Jeff Stone

Random House New York

Text copyright © 2010 by Jeffrey S. Stone
Jacket art copyright © 2010 by Richard Cowdrey

Published in the United States by Random House Children's Books, a division of Random House, Inc., New York.

Random House and the colophon are registered trademarks of Random House, Inc.

The Five Ancestors is a registered trademark of Jeffrey S. Stone.

Visit us on the Web! www.randomhouse.com/kids

Educators and librarians, for a variety of teaching tools, visit us at www.randomhouse.com/teachers

www.fiveancestors.com

Library of Congress Cataloging-in-Publication Data
Stone, Jeff.
Dragon / Jeff Stone. — 1st ed.
    p.   cm. — (The five ancestors ; bk. 7)
Summary: Thirteen-year-old Long, a dragon-style kung fu master and the oldest of the five survivors of the destroyed Cangzhen, must get to the Forbidden City before Tonglong declares himself emperor.
ISBN 978-0-375-83079-2 (trade) — ISBN 978-0-375-93079-9 (lib. bdg.) — ISBN 978-0-375-89319-3 (e-book) — ISBN 978-0-375-83080-8 (pbk.)
[1. Martial arts—Fiction. 2. Human-animal relationships—Fiction.
3. China—History—1644–1795—Fiction.] I. Title.
PZ7.S87783Dr 2010   [Fic]—dc22   2009032416

Printed in the United States of America

10 9 8 7 6 5 4 3 2 1

First Edition

for Jim Thomas,

for getting me started;
and for R. Schuyler Hooke,

for showing me the way home

THE FIVE ANCESTORS

龍 Dragon

Jeff Stone

Henan Province, China
4348 – Year of the Tiger
(1650 AD)

Thirteen-year-old Long limped along the Shanghai Fight Club tunnel, a river of blood flowing down his right thigh, the weight of a nation on his shoulders. He glanced at the crimson liquid oozing from his bandaged leg, and the steady stream leaking from his upper left arm.

So much for winning the Fight Club Grand Championship. Previous champions had earned themselves prime positions within the Emperor's military ranks. Long had earned himself a target on his head.

Balanced across Long's powerful shoulders was the unconscious giant of a man known as Xie—the Scorpion. Xie had been the Emperor's personal bodyguard, but as of a quarter of an hour ago, he was, like Long, a fugitive.

Long had to keep moving. Soldiers would surely be racing after them, following the directions of the new Southern Warlord—Tonglong, the Mantis. However, Long had no time to consider them or their whereabouts. He had a more pressing matter to deal with. He needed to lower his pulse. If he kept going at this pace, his racing heart would soon pump his body dry.

Long—the Dragon—began a breathing sequence that would decrease his heart rate in order to slow his blood flow. Two short breaths in, one long one out. He felt a difference immediately.

He continued along the tunnel's dirt floor, but a stirring sensation in his *dan tien*—his *chi* center—brought a sudden sense of dread. His lower abdomen began to warm and his intestines started writhing like a ball of snakes. Someone was coming.

"Golden Dragon?" a tiny voice whispered from down the dark corridor behind him. "Long? Are you there?"

Long stopped and frowned. It was ShaoShu—Little Mouse. ShaoShu had used Long's fight club name: Golden Dragon. Long turned and watched the small boy with the unusually limber body scamper toward him from the direction he had come from.

"Turn back, ShaoShu," Long whispered. "Return to Tonglong. You will not be safe with me."

"I don't care," ShaoShu replied. "I want to help. You're injured and— Hey!" he squeaked, pointing at Xie. "Xie is alive! His arm just moved. How can that be? I watched Tonglong shoot him in the chest."

"Xie is wearing battle armor beneath his robe," Long said. "The shock from Tonglong's bullet just knocked him out. He probably has a cracked rib or two, but that's it. He should be fine once he wakes up."

ShaoShu stared at Long's bulging arms and thick chest. "You're carrying him *and* battle armor? You're barely a man. How did you get so strong?"

"Exercise," Long replied. "Now shoo."

"But I can help," ShaoShu said. "Did you see what happened back there with the Emperor and Tonglong? You can't do this alone."

"I saw," Long said. "Tonglong killed Xie's father—the Western Warlord. He also killed his own mother, AnGangseh. He's crazy, but he has managed to put himself in a position to kidnap the Emperor, and that makes him dangerous and powerful."

"Crazy is right," ShaoShu said. "He will kill you, too, if you're caught. Why are you carrying Xie around? Just leave him. He's always been mean to you."

"If my temple brothers and sisters are to have any chance of stopping Tonglong from taking over the country, we are going to need Xie's help. He is still a very powerful man. In fact, he is the Western Warlord now. He—"

Long stopped in midsentence as he saw ShaoShu's body go rigid and his nose twitch.

"Uh-oh," ShaoShu said.

Long focused his attention down the dark fight club tunnel beyond ShaoShu, and his *dan tien* began to twist and turn. More people were coming.

"Listen," Long whispered to ShaoShu. "You must either return to Tonglong right now or escape on your own. You can't stay with me."

"What are you going to do?"

"I will get Xie to safety, then I will rendezvous with my brothers and sister far to the north. Now go."

Long whirled around to leave, but his foot slipped in a pool of his own blood. He lost his balance, and Xie's gigantic body shifted across his shoulders, dragging him to one side. His injured leg collapsed, and he went down. Xie's head bounced off the tunnel wall, the impact waking him instantly.

Xie sat up, fully alert, like a seasoned fighter who had been knocked out only to wake up swinging.

"What is going on?" Xie demanded, staggering to his feet. He tottered, then centered himself and stood solid as a mountain. He rubbed his head with one hand and felt the dent in his chest plate with the other.

"We're being hunted," Long said. He watched as first recognition and then memory flowed behind Xie's eyes.

Xie growled and glared back up the tunnel.

Long spun around to see two soldiers approaching, one tall and one short. Each held a cocked pistol. The soldiers stopped just out of Long's and Xie's reach. The taller of the two cleared his throat.

"Our apologies, sir," the taller soldier said to Xie, "but you are under arrest. Southern Warlord Tonglong has ordered us to capture you, as well as Golden Dragon. Both of you, please come with us and maintain a reasonable distance. Our orders are to take you dead or alive. We will not hesitate to shoot either of you if you come too close or attempt to flee."

Long's heart sank. In a traditional scuffle they might stand a chance, but against firearms combined with a short distance, all the kung fu skills on the planet would not help. He looked over to see ShaoShu's reaction, but ShaoShu was gone.

Long was about to look back at Xie when he noticed a blur of movement behind the taller soldier. It seemed ShaoShu hadn't gone very far.

ShaoShu scurried out of the shadows and sank his teeth into the taller soldier's right calf. The soldier howled and spun around, swinging the butt of his heavy pistol at ShaoShu's head. ShaoShu flattened himself enough to avoid the blow.

The shorter soldier glanced sideways at his partner to see what was the matter, and in that instant Xie struck. Long had never seen a man as large as him move so fast. Xie covered the distance between himself and the second soldier with a lightning-quick shuffle-step and brought a hammer fist down onto the bridge of the soldier's nose so hard that Long heard the man's face crack.

The shorter soldier dropped. He would not be getting up again.

The taller soldier straightened and leveled his pistol at Xie, and Long sprang into action. He leaped with his good left leg and landed in a crouch on his left foot, just out of the taller soldier's reach. Long whipped his body around, raising his damaged right leg and slamming it into the outside of the soldier's right knee with the force of a dragon whipping its tail.

The soldier screamed as his knee *popped!*, and Long grimaced as the gash in his own leg grew wider. Long's eyes began to water, and through the tears he saw Xie drive an elbow into the side of the taller soldier's head. This man would not be getting up again, either.

Xie kicked the soldiers aside and knelt next to Long. "Thank you. I may owe you my life."

"It was nothing," Long replied in a weary tone.

"Are you okay?" Xie asked. "Your face is deathly pale. I believe you may have lost a lot of blood. Let me carry you, Golden Dragon."

Long's pride wanted to refuse the offer, but his common sense accepted it. He was feeling light-headed. "Thank *you*," he said. "But please call me Long. That is my real name. Golden Dragon is dead."

"As you wish."

Xie scooped Long into his arms, and Long looked down to see ShaoShu picking bits of silk pant leg from his teeth.

ShaoShu grinned. "How did I do?"

Xie chuckled. "I had never heard of mouse-style kung fu before tonight. Well done, little one."

"Yes, very well done," Long said.

ShaoShu beamed.

"Could you do me a favor, ShaoShu?" Xie asked. "Place the soldiers' pistols in my sash."

"Sure," ShaoShu said. He hurriedly picked up the

pistols, uncocked them, and tucked them behind Xie's wide sash. Then he looked at Long. "I'd better get back to Tonglong before he becomes suspicious. I will continue spying on him, though, and I'll try to figure out a way to get information to you."

"I still think you should run away," Long said weakly, "but I am too tired to argue. Be careful, and do not stay with Tonglong any longer than you have to. You do remember how to find Hok and the others, right?"

"Of course," ShaoShu replied. "Go to the Jade Phoenix restaurant in the city of Kaifeng. Ask for Yuen."

"That's right," Long said. "Thanks, ShaoShu."

"Yes, many thanks, Little Mouse," Xie added.

ShaoShu smiled and disappeared down the tunnel.

Long sighed and looked at Xie. He had never felt so exhausted. "There is an exit ahead. Are you familiar with it?"

"I am. Let's go."

Xie pushed forward through the tunnel with Long bleeding in his arms. He kept to the shadows and moved like his scorpion namesake, sure of himself yet cautious around every bend, every doorway. Long reached out as often as he could, extinguishing torches that were hanging along the tunnel's stone walls, in order to put a buffer between them and any trouble on their flank. It slowed their forward progress but appeared to be worth the effort. No one caught up with them, and they reached the exit safely.

Long groaned softly as Xie rested him on the tunnel's

dirt floor. Xie remained silent as he knelt down to make his gigantic self as inconspicuous as possible, then opened the exit door and poked his head outside.

"I don't see anyone," Xie whispered. "Tonglong must still be in the process of shutting down the perimeter. We should make a run for it."

"Let me see," Long whispered.

Xie leaned back inside, and Long repositioned himself to face the door. Even that little effort made Long swoon. He carefully stuck his head into the cool night air and found that the moon was bright. Xie appeared to be right. The area looked vacant.

Long pulled his head inside. "What if they have snipers on the rooftops?"

"We will have to take our chances. They may not have had time to do that yet. It is my guess that Tonglong is busy with other things. Locating us is secondary to his larger objectives. He will deal with the Emperor first."

Long heard tension in Xie's voice, and he thought again about what he had seen earlier. Tonglong had killed two people in cold blood.

Long shivered. "I am sorry about your father."

Xie gnashed his teeth. "Tonglong is the one who will be sorry."

Long did not doubt Xie. He leaned through the doorway again and felt his *dan tien* begin to quiver. There was someone out there. He attempted to scan the rooftops and found that his vision was blurring from fatigue and blood loss. He strained to focus in the moonlight, but it was no use.

"Do you see anything?" Long asked. "My eyesight is fading."

Xie carefully stood and leaned over Long, looking outside. "Yes!" Xie replied. "I see something on one of the nearby roofs. It appears to be a . . ." His voice trailed off.

"Appears to be what?" Long asked.

"Call me crazy, but it looks like a monkey jumping up and down, waving its arms."

Long felt a glimmer of hope. "Is the monkey alone?"

"I believe so. It is partially in shadow, and . . . wait! There *is* someone else. A woman, or maybe a tall girl. She is wearing a white dress and a white turban. She glided out of the moon shadows beside the monkey for the briefest of moments, then nodded in our direction and retreated. If I were superstitious, I would have guessed that she was a ghost. I have never seen a human move that gracefully."

Long smiled, his own world now draped in shadows. "Pick me up and run to them as quickly as you can. It seems there is hope for us yet."

And then Long blacked out.

CHAPTER 2

"ShaoShu!" Tonglong snapped. "Where have you been? I was about to send a search party after you."

ShaoShu hurried out of the Shanghai Fight Club tunnel and stopped before twenty-nine-year-old Tonglong, who was standing inside the fight club's main rear exit. ShaoShu struggled to catch his breath. "I got lost, sir," he lied. "I am very sorry. Are we going somewhere?"

"We are indeed," Tonglong said. "All the way to the Forbidden City. Come with me."

Tonglong flipped his extraordinarily long, thick ponytail braid forward over his shoulder, securing its tip to his sash. He headed toward a group of four soldiers waiting outside the exit door. The men wore the red silk robes and pants of Tonglong's elite Southern army uniform, and they carried a large object wrapped in a blanket. ShaoShu realized that there was a person inside it, wrapped up like an egg roll.

"Is this how you plan to transport the cargo?" Tonglong asked as he stepped through the doorway, into the night.

"Yes, sir," one of the soldiers replied.

"Well done."

ShaoShu reached the exit door and saw a donkey attached to a cart. Next to the cart was a filthy rectangular wooden crate. Ventilation holes had been drilled at regular intervals along the upper section of each side, and large hinges were affixed to one of the sides and a heavy hasp to the opposite. Judging from the smell, ShaoShu guessed that the crate had once held pigs.

"I believe it is large enough," the soldier said to Tonglong, "but not everyone agrees with me."

"Find out," Tonglong said. "Open it."

The men did as ordered, and Tonglong stepped around to the far side of the crate to get a closer look inside. The soldiers stepped around, too, and began to manhandle their squirming parcel to see how it might fit inside the crate. A section of the wrapping came loose, and ShaoShu saw a flash of brilliant yellow silk. This confirmed what he had suspected. Only one person in all of China was allowed to wear the color yellow, and it was the Emperor. Yellow symbolized the Emperor's divine connection with the sun.

ShaoShu felt no great devotion to the Emperor, but he did feel sorry for anyone who was being mistreated. He turned away from the spectacle and noticed something moving very fast and low to the ground in the distance. On first glance, it appeared to be a large shadow. However, after staring hard, ShaoShu realized that it had to be Xie and Long!

He watched out of the corner of his eye as they crossed the open ground and slipped undetected behind a building. ShaoShu glanced back at Tonglong and the soldiers, but they were still occupied with the Emperor.

ShaoShu risked looking over toward Xie and Long once more. He saw a figure appear to float over to the edge of the building's rooftop. It was Hok! She turned toward him, and he pointed to the wrapped captive. Hok seemed to nod, then she simply disappeared.

ShaoShu grinned and looked back at the group of soldiers. One of them glared at him. "What is so funny?"

"Uh, nothing, sir," ShaoShu replied nervously. He realized that his arm was still outstretched, and he lowered it.

Tonglong looked at him from the far side of the pig crate. "What were you pointing at?"

ShaoShu's eyes fixed upon the patch of yellow showing from within the captive's wrapping, and one of the soldiers laughed out loud.

"That *is* pretty funny, isn't it?" the man said. "We confiscated the Emperor's robes, which means even his underpants are yellow!" The soldier chuckled, and he quickly rearranged the blankets to cover the yellow cloth. Even Tonglong grinned.

ShaoShu turned away. He really did not feel much like laughing. Behind him, he heard the Emperor being loaded into the pig crate, and something that sounded like a huge padlock being put through a hasp.

A commotion within the fight club caught ShaoShu's attention, and he looked over to see two soldiers running toward Tonglong and the soldiers. Unlike the four soldiers standing next to the cart, these men wore black silk robes with blue pants. They were the Eastern Warlord's soldiers.

The two newcomers stepped into the moonlight and bowed before Tonglong. One of them said, "We have news, sir."

"Yes?" Tonglong said.

"Let me start by saying that it is an honor to serve you, sir. We have been informed that our Eastern Warlord has relinquished his command to you."

Tonglong nodded, and the man continued.

"I regret that I must report that we have been unable to locate Golden Dragon or Xie's body. In fact, evidence has been found that leads us to believe Xie may still be alive."

Tonglong's eyebrows rose in surprise. "Still alive? What evidence?"

"There was an attack in the tunnels, sir. Two of our men were found dead. The site was littered with footprints the size of Xie's."

"But I shot him in the chest."

"Yes, sir. Xie was known to wear body armor beneath his robes."

Tonglong ground his teeth. "I see. I presume you have men looking for him, as well as Golden Dragon?"

"We do, sir. More than a hundred of our soldiers are combing the fight club at this very moment."

"Keep me apprised."

"Of course, sir."

Tonglong spat, and some of his spittle hit the second Eastern soldier's boot. The man jumped back, a look of disgust on his face.

Tonglong glared at the man, and the man's expression changed to one of fear. He began to shuffle his feet nervously.

"Is there a problem?" Tonglong asked.

The second soldier straightened. "No, sir!"

"Are you sure?"

"Yes, sir."

"Well, I believe there is," Tonglong said. "If you flinch like that over a little spit, how will you react when blood begins to spill?"

"Excuse me, sir?"

Tonglong's eyes narrowed. "How many battles have you been a part of?"

The man looked confused. "None, sir. We have had only peace in this region for more than a hundred years."

Tonglong gripped the hilt of his straight sword. "Then perhaps I need to help you Eastern soldiers grow accustomed to bloodshed."

"I apologize, sir," the soldier said. "I—"

The man's words were cut short by the sound of Tonglong's straight sword slicing through the air. His blade moved faster and more powerfully than ShaoShu could have imagined. It breezed clean through the soldier's head as though it were nothing more than an overripe peach, splattering blood across the torso of the first soldier.

The second soldier dropped in a lifeless heap, and ShaoShu fought back a shriek. Tonglong's sword had gone from sheath to killing blow in the blink of an eye.

Tonglong turned to the first soldier, and the man dropped to his knees.

"Please spare me, sir," the soldier said in a quivering voice.

"Shut up," Tonglong said. "On your feet."

The soldier stood.

"Tell your Eastern comrades what you have seen here. Show them the stains on your uniform. Let none of them say that they have never seen another man's blood."

"Yes, sir!"

"Now get out of here and find those fugitives!"

The soldier hurried away, and Tonglong knelt beside the fallen Eastern soldier. He calmly began to wipe his blade on the dead man's robe. He worked with the emotionless precision of an insect, reminding ShaoShu of a mantis cleaning its forelegs after a kill.

ShaoShu shivered. Who could possibly stop Tonglong?

CHAPTER 3

Four hundred *li* southwest of Shanghai, Ying sat alone beneath a mountain pine tree, his eyes closed tight, his mind open wide. Legend said that it took more than three thousand years for a dragon to grow to realize its deadliest potential. Ying guessed that he had about a month.

Tonglong would be on the move soon, and he needed to be ready for him.

With his legs folded beneath him and his hands upon his knees, Ying meditated. He focused his attention on his *dan tien,* the mysterious *chi* center in his lower abdomen, and began to breathe in a specific rhythm that his mother had taught him. In no time, he felt *chi* circulating through his body, rippling in waves, warming everything from the tips of his long fingernails and toenails to the pigmented scar tissue carved into his face. He had to admit, it felt good.

Ying exhaled slowly, enjoying the sensation, and found himself thinking about his mother. She was resting nearby at a friend's house. He had come out here at her urging so that he could prepare himself for his inevitable confrontation with Tonglong. As so often was the case, her idea had been a good one. Thanks to the breathing exercises she had taught him and the powdered dragon bone he had been consuming, he now truly felt like a dragon instead of the eagle his name—Ying—implied.

Ying opened his eyes and felt his inner *chi* flow begin to dissipate as he eased himself out of his meditative state. Mountains filled his vision in every direction, and he grinned. He was at home. There were several different types of Chinese dragons, and they ruled everything from the seas to the rivers to the skies. Some dragons even protected treasure hordes like the one Tonglong had stolen from Ying's family. Ying, however, was a mountain dragon through and through.

Mountain dragons, like all Chinese dragons, were impressive creatures. They were made up of the strongest elements of many different animals, which is what made them—and dragon-style kung fu—so powerful. Dragons were primarily serpentine in shape, but they possessed four legs, each ending with a set of talons. These talons came from an eagle, but the pads of the feet were those of a tiger.

Chinese dragons also had spindly whiskers like a carp, plus a long beard that was more like a mustache. The longer the mustache, the older the dragon. Some people even believed that a very thick mustache meant the dragon was extraordinarily wise. Finally, Chinese dragons possessed the antlers of a deer and, most striking of all, the eyes of a demon.

Ying fixed his eyes on the forest floor and stood. He rubbed his chilly bare hands together to get his blood flowing and set his mind to thinking about Tonglong. It was time for some physical training.

Tonglong was a master of the straight sword, and if Ying had any hopes of defeating him, he would have to fight fire with fire. Tonglong's guards would never let anyone get within pistol or even musket range of Tonglong, but Tonglong would welcome a straight sword challenge from anyone, including Ying. He was that good.

While Ying was proficient with edged weapons, he was no match for Tonglong. Even Ying's weapon of choice, an extra-long chain whip, likely would not get the job done. However, Ying had heard rumors back when he lived at Cangzhen Temple about a combined straight sword and chain whip sequence that was supposedly unbeatable. The practitioner used both weapons simultaneously, one in each hand. This allowed him to take advantage of the chain's long-range capabilities, as well as the sword's short-range precision. It also coupled the rigidity of the sword with the flexibility of the chain. It was the best of the hard and the soft, the yin and the yang.

This special two-weapon sequence was rumored to be recorded in one of the Cangzhen Temple dragon scrolls, but Ying had never seen it. He had managed to get his hands on most of the scrolls, but he had lost possession of them. He would have to try to develop a sequence himself.

Ying scanned the ground, and his eyes soon fell upon what he was seeking—a perfectly straight branch about as long as his arm and half as thick as his wrist at one end. The opposite end tapered to the width of his thumb. Perfect.

Ying lifted the branch by the fat end and measured its weight in his left hand. It would do nicely. He slipped his chain whip out of the hidden pocket in the inside of the sleeve of his robe, gripping its rigid handle with his right hand. He began to swing the multisection steel weapon powerfully over his head, like a man attempting to catch an animal with a rope.

The sharp, weighted tip of the chain whip sliced through the air, severing pine boughs and tree limbs in every direction. He continued until he had cleared a wide circle that would allow him to swing his chain whip any way he chose without interference. Then he began to create a deadly new dance.

Between long, slashing swings of the chain whip, Ying thrust his practice branch forward again and again. The chain connected with the end of the branch more often than not, and in no time he was left with a short practice dagger as opposed to a long practice sword.

Ying tossed the stubby stick aside and looked

around the forest floor once more, this time gathering an armload of branches that would serve his purpose. This was going to take time. He would give himself two weeks to practice, and another two weeks to find himself a real sword. Then he would have to locate Tonglong and face his destiny.

Long heard the voice as if in a dream. The accent was odd, but the words were definitely Chinese.

"Put on all she can wear, mateys! We can do this! The wind is in our favor!"

Long forced his eyes open and found himself lying flat on his back, the ground rolling and pitching violently beneath him. The sun was high overhead, and the crisp scent of salt water invaded his nostrils. He was in a boat.

But whose boat was it? And what day was it?

Long rolled onto his side and tried to raise himself up onto one elbow to take a look around. He'd made it halfway there when his arm slipped on the boat's slick deck, and he flopped back down with a groan, dizzy.

"He's awake!" a familiar voice shrieked from somewhere nearby.

Long raised his head, tilting it left and then right. Strangely, he did not see anyone. Then he gazed up. At the very top of the boat's single tall mast, he saw Malao's dark-skinned face beaming down at him.

Long grinned.

Malao raised a hand and waved, seemingly oblivious to the fact that his perch was swinging wildly back and forth through a full ninety degrees of motion as the boat rolled in the wind-driven seas. "Hello, Big Brother!" Malao shouted down to him.

Long nodded a greeting and mustered as much strength as he could, struggling again to lift himself onto his elbow. This time, he succeeded. He glanced over the side of the boat and saw that they were tearing along at an impressive rate. He'd had no idea a boat could move so fast.

"Lie down, Brother," urged a gentle voice behind him. A moment later, his younger temple sister, Hok, appeared at his side. She took his wrist in her hand, searching for his pulse.

Long glanced at Hok's smooth pale skin and spiky brown hair. He had learned from Grandmaster that Hok had a Chinese mother and a Dutch father. That accounted for her light skin, but he had never seen her with hair. It looked nice, but made her look as out of place as she had probably felt growing up pretending to be a boy.

"Conserve your energy," Hok said to him. "Charles has everything under control."

"Charles?" Long asked.

Someone began to grumble from the front of the boat. "*Charles* has everything under control? Hmpf."

Long smiled as he recognized that deep, complaining voice. He glanced at the boat's bow and saw Fu expertly rearranging a complicated series of ropes. Fu was shirtless despite the cold weather, and Long was surprised to see how much Fu had thinned out, and how much muscle mass he had gained. Fu's chest might have been even larger than his own, which really was impressive considering Long had the build of an eighteen-year-old and Fu was only twelve.

"Hello, Fu," Long called out in as loud a voice as he could manage.

"Ahoy," Fu replied. "I would come over to say hello, but I'm kind of busy right now. I'm helping *Charles*."

Long wondered if Fu might stalk over to wherever this Charles was standing in order to give Charles a piece of his mind, or possibly a piece of his fist. Instead, Fu did the strangest thing. He laughed. Then he shouted, "Sorry, Charles. I'm only teasing."

Long blinked. What had happened to Fu? The Fu he knew never apologized for anything.

Things grew even stranger when Long twisted his head around toward the back of the boat. Behind the ship's wheel stood a white teenage boy with straw-colored hair and eyes the color of the sea. Towering next to him was Xie.

Xie clapped the foreign teenager on the shoulder and said, "We are in fine hands, Long. This is Charles. Or should I say, Captain Charles?"

Charles smiled warmly and nodded to Long. "Nice to finally meet you. Welcome aboard."

"Thank you," Long replied. He felt Hok release his wrist, and he turned his attention back to her.

"Please lie down," Hok said. "You need to conserve your energy. Your pulse is very faint and you have lost a lot of blood. You are lucky to be alive. It took more than one hundred stitches to close your wounds, and I had to sew them while the boat was moving. It is not my best work. Some of them are bound to split open if you do not lie still."

Long knew firsthand his sister's gifts as a healer, and he obeyed without question, lying back down on the boat's rolling deck. Her handiwork had impressed everyone at Cangzhen Temple, and she had patched him up more than once after training sessions that had gone awry. He noticed now that his right thigh and the upper section of his left arm had been expertly rebandaged. That was no doubt her doing, too. He asked, "What is going on? I cannot seem to remember much."

"There is quite a bit going on," Hok replied. "Why don't you tell me what you know, first?"

"From the beginning?"

"Sure."

"Well," Long said, "six months ago, Ying attacked our Cangzhen Temple with the aid of the Emperor's soldiers. They had firearms and cannons, while we had swords and spears. Only Fu, Malao, Seh, you, and I managed to survive. I thought that Grandmaster might have made it out, too, but I later learned that Ying had killed him as well."

"Go on."

"I fled the attack as Grandmaster had commanded, and I came up with the idea of joining the fight clubs like Ying had done, in order to get close to the Emperor. I thought I might be able to change the Emperor's heart like Grandmaster had directed us. I did manage to get close to the Emperor and even succeeded in becoming this year's Fight Club Grand Champion, but it was all for naught. As Xie has probably told you, Tonglong is now the Southern Warlord, and he made a move against the Emperor right after I won the championship. I believe he may have succeeded. This is all I know."

Hok nodded. "Unfortunately, I think you are correct about Tonglong succeeding. I saw ShaoShu briefly as we were leaving the rooftop across from the fight club last night, and he pointed to a figure wrapped in some sort of blanket, held by soldiers. A section of the blanket had separated, and in the moonlight I saw a flash of gold silk."

"So I have only been asleep one night?"

"Yes."

"And ShaoShu is definitely back with Tonglong?"

"Yes."

"I wish he would have come with us."

"ShaoShu can take care of himself," Hok said. "What more can I tell you about our situation?"

Long glanced at Charles, then back at Hok. "Tell me about this fine boat."

"The boat belongs to Charles, of course," Hok replied. "He is a friend of my father and my mother, and I am proud to call him my friend, too. I believe we all are."

Fu grunted in agreement from the bow, and Malao shouted down from the mast top, "Hear, hear!"

Hok continued. "Charles has been helping us for a while now, and we have been keeping an eye on Tonglong. We were recently staying with a group of Charles' friends on a small island to the south, but Tonglong found us and destroyed everything and nearly everyone. We were fortunate to escape. Charles was going to take us farther north so that we could meet up with Seh and a group of bandits he is staying with."

"Bandits?" Long asked. "Are you talking about Mong?"

Hok's eyebrows rose. "Yes. How do you know about Mong?"

"Grandmaster shared some secrets with me," Long said, slightly embarrassed. "Do you know that there is history between Mong and Seh?"

Hok nodded. "Yes, Mong is Seh's father."

"That's right."

"Do you know anything about Seh's mother?"

"No."

"His mother is, or I should say was, AnGangseh."

Long shook his head. "AnGangseh was Tonglong's mother."

"She is mother to both of them, though from different husbands. Seh and Tonglong are half-brothers."

"Unbelievable," Long said.

"There is more," Hok said. "AnGangseh blinded

Seh. That is why he is not traveling with us." She tapped the side of her ever-present herb bag. "Fortunately, I may have found a cure in the form of dragon bone. Now that you are with us, we are hurrying to Seh and the bandits. Fu's father is with them, too, as is my mother and hopefully my little sister."

"I feel bad for Seh," Long said. "Did you say that you have a sister?"

"Yes. I only learned of her when I reunited with my mother. Besides my family, we have also tried to find information about Malao's father, a man known as the Monkey King, but no one seems to have seen him in years. Fu has reunited with his father, though. His name is Sanfu—Mountain Tiger."

"It sounds like you have been busy," Long said, feeling light-headed. "What about Ying? I have heard rumors about him, but I do not know what is fact and what is fiction."

Hok smiled. "You are never going to believe all that has happened with him. He is no longer the same person. We consider him an ally. He had a life-changing reunion with his mother and learned some startling things about his father, and especially his grandfather."

Long's eyes widened. "Ying knows about his grandfather?"

"Yes," Hok said. "Grandmaster was Ying's grandfather. Isn't that tragic? Although he did not know it at the time, when Ying killed Grandmaster, he killed his only living relative besides his mother."

Long closed his eyes, his dizziness worsening. "That is not exactly true."

"What do you mean?"

"Ying has at least one more living relative, though his health is questionable at the moment."

"Who?

"Me."

"What?" Fu roared from the bow of Charles' boat. "You and Ying are related?"

Long sighed. "You have good ears, Fu. Yes, Grandmaster was also my grandfather. Ying and I are cousins."

"Does Ying know this?" Hok asked.

"I do not believe so," Long replied. "Grandmaster kept many secrets, especially from Ying. It seems Ying's father and my father were brothers. I always wanted to tell Ying, but Grandmaster forbade me. One thing Ying did know, though, was that Grandmaster killed his father. Ying was very young, but he saw it happen and he never forgot. I believe this is the main reason he killed Grandmaster—revenge. Additionally, Ying was upset that Grandmaster had changed his name. Ying's name used to be Saulong—Vengeful Dragon. Grandmaster changed his name and started teaching him eagle-style kung fu instead of dragon-style."

"That would upset me, too," Charles said.

Long nodded.

"Wait—" Hok said. "If Grandmaster killed Ying's father, that would mean that Grandmaster killed his own son."

"That's right," Long said, his voice faltering. "Grandmaster told me that he did it after Ying's father killed *my* parents. Grandmaster said that he had two sons, a good son—my father—and a bad son, Ying's father. Grandmaster told me that Ying's father was an abomination and needed to be dealt with so that no more people would be hurt by him. He said that the negative traits of a dragon were somehow amplified in Ying's father, and he feared that Ying might be the same way. That is why he raised Ying as an eagle."

"This is awful," Hok said.

"It is," Long said. "Poor Ying. I do not know anything about his mother, who would be my aunt."

"We have met her," Hok said. "Her name is WanSow—Cloud Hand—and she is a wonderful person. She was injured by Tonglong, but Ying is taking care of her now."

"It sounds like Ying really has changed," Long said. Hok nodded.

"I hope to see him again," Long said. "My aunt WanSow, too. If you happen to see him without me, please tell him all that I have shared with you. He needs to know. Grandmaster kept too many secrets. Look where it has gotten us."

Hok nodded again, and a weary grin crept across Long's face. After all that he and his temple siblings had been through, it seemed everyone was doing all right. The only exception might be Seh.

As the heavy hands of unconsciousness began to

press against Long's mind once more, he closed his eyes and thought about his blind brother. Losing one's sight was a fate worse than death for some people, and it would spell the end for most creatures in the wild.

Long wondered how a snake would handle it.

Twelve-year-old Seh stood before the line of bandit recruits, a razor-sharp spear in one hand, a teacup in the other. He raised the cup to his lips, swallowing the wretched contents in one gulp. He gagged briefly, but managed to keep the medicine down.

One of the recruits scoffed. "What are you going to teach us, young *sifu*? How to distract an opponent by puking on him?"

A few of the recruits chuckled, and Seh frowned. It was like this with every new group. This particular bunch consisted of fifteen men between the ages of twenty and thirty-five. He was going to have to earn their respect, and that usually meant confrontation. His vision was far from functional, but he could now

THE
FIVE
ANCESTORS

see shadows and had learned to identify individuals by the unique amounts of positive or negative energy they generated. The joker stood in the center of the line, radiating negative energy like a furnace.

One of the recruits spoke up in Seh's defense. "Give our young instructor some respect, gentlemen. He is blind, and he drinks powdered dragon bone in an attempt to regain his sight. Have you ever tried it? It is horrible."

"Dragon bone, eh?" the joker said. "He must be a spoiled rich kid to be able to afford such expensive medicine. I guess that is how it works when you are Mong's son."

Seh felt anger begin to rise within him, but he fought off the urge to be rude. He decided to give the men a short explanation to try to ease the growing tension. Then he would move on with teaching the class.

"The dragon bone was a gift from a black market dealer called HukJee—Black Pig," Seh told the group. "HukJee learned that some friends of mine were looking for dragon bone, and a healer friend of our camp named PawPaw realized that dragon bone might be able to help me with my condition. It is true that I have lost my sight, but it has been returning more each week. Today's lesson will be that vision isn't everything. I can use other senses to defeat opponents."

"Like your sense of taste?" the joker asked. "To help with your projectile vomiting?"

The same recruits laughed, and Seh wondered how

men more than twice his age found these childish comments funny.

Seh turned away from the group and walked under a large tent frame that had not been covered with fabric. He could vaguely discern the outlines of several round clay pots hanging at different heights from the crossbeams. The pots were filled with sand, and dangling from the bottom of each was a square sheet of metal roughly the size of his hand.

Seh subconsciously pushed a lock of his fast-growing hair out of his mostly sightless eyes and pointed more or less in the direction of the man who had spoken up for him. It was time for a little demonstration.

"Please, come here," Seh said.

The man came forward, and Seh nodded toward the pots. "I want you to hit each of those dangling sheets of metal, then get out of the way as quickly as you can."

"Okay," the man replied.

Seh heard five distinct *clangs,* and the moment he saw the man's shadowy form hurry off to one side, he sprang into action. He rushed forward, swinging his iron-tipped spear in a wide swath, smashing three of the pots in dramatic fashion on the first pass. He felt the satisfying *thunk* as the clay vessels exploded, and registered the distinctive *hiss* of sand flying through the air.

He keyed in on the faint tones emitted by the two remaining metal sheets, and he went after them with all the focus of a kung fu master. He thrust the spear tip at one of the pots, shattering it. Then he pulled his spear back as though to smash the remaining pot, but instead snapped his right foot forward, shouting, "Ki-ya!"

It was a direct hit. The ball of his foot connected with the final pot, and the pot erupted, sending a shower of hardened clay fragments and sand in every direction as the metal sheet dropped to the ground.

Seh landed on his knees for show, his spear held high over his head. He jumped to his feet, bowed quickly to the line of men, and began to dust himself off.

Several of the recruits murmured their approval. The joker scoffed. "I'll be sure to remember this lesson if I'm ever blindfolded and attacked by a troop of killer flowerpots."

"Is there something you would like to discuss?" Seh asked the joker.

"Yeah," the joker replied. "I want to know why you are wasting our time. Breaking pots serves no purpose."

"That is not true," Seh said. "Those pots are the same diameter as a human head, and they are hung at different levels to represent opponents of different heights. The force required to shatter one when it is filled with sand is the same amount of force necessary to crack a human skull. It is important practice."

The joker laughed. "Pots don't fight back, young man. People do. People also move around. A person would simply get out of your way."

Seh clenched his teeth. "Would *you* like to try it?"

"Attack some harmless flowerpots?"

"No. Attempt to get out of my way."

The joker's tone grew serious. "Are you saying that you want to fight me, boy?"

"I prefer the term *sparring*," Seh said. "Unless you are afraid, old man."

"Old man!" the joker roared. "I'll show you!"

Seh heard the man's heavy boots begin to pound across the ground in his direction. It did not surprise him that the joker acted so spontaneously. In fact, he had been counting on it. Embarrassing this man here and now would earn Seh the respect of the entire group.

Seh sank into a deep Horse Stance and gripped his spear with two hands, holding the wooden shaft parallel to the ground with the metal tip facing forward. He held the shaft's center balance point tight in his left hand at waist level and positioned his right hand near the blunt back end.

He had no idea whether the joker had a weapon, but was certain that he would prevail as long as his opponent did not carry pistols. Seh heard metal unsheathed, and from the sound determined that the man possessed a broadsword of moderate length. No problem.

The joker continued his charge, and when Seh could hear the man's intense breathing, he knew that his opponent was close enough.

Seh struck. He kept his left hand locked and thrust

his right hand downward in a large half-circle. This caused the tip of the spear to rise up in an opposing half-circle, heading directly for the joker's face. The joker chopped down at the spear tip with his broadsword, just as Seh expected he would, and the broadsword made contact with the spear tip, redirecting the spear tip down toward the ground.

As the spear tip continued its downward motion, Seh thrust it forward, accurately visualizing the spear passing between the man's legs. Seh clamped the spear shaft in his armpit and rolled to one side, yanking the spear sideways. The spear shaft tangled the man's legs, and he tripped hard and fell to the ground, face-first.

Seh dropped the spear and was about to slither onto the joker's back for a choke hold when someone shouted, "Enough!"

Seh froze. He felt the air behind him begin to pulse with restrained aggression. He did not have to turn around to know that his father was approaching.

"Did you hurt him?" Mong asked as he stopped next to Seh.

Seh fixed his gaze in the general direction of his downed opponent. "How should I know?"

"Good point," Mong said, slapping Seh on the shoulder. "Nice move, by the way." Seh felt the aggression within his father begin to dissipate.

Seh nodded, and he heard the joker groan.

"He looks like he is going to be fine," Mong said. "Listen, I realize that sometimes you need to make an example of someone, but next time please try to pick a younger man. He looks to be in his mid-thirties, and older individuals, like myself, take longer to heal. I fear we are going to need all the extra hands we can get very soon."

"I will remember," Seh said. "Have you received some news?"

"Yes. It is all speculation at this point, but we believe that Tonglong may attempt to amass an army."

"What does that mean?"

"It means that you are going to have to train more men," Mong said. "A lot more."

CHAPTER 6

ShaoShu sat obediently inside the door of Tonglong's central command office on the outskirts of Shanghai. He was sitting absolutely still, trying not to be noticed. Across the room, Tonglong was in a furious mood, and it looked like things were about to get worse.

"Sign and seal it!" Tonglong ordered.

The Emperor folded his arms. "No."

Tonglong slammed his fist against the heavy oak desk, scattering a series of scrolls. A bowl of ink tumbled over, and ShaoShu watched the black liquid seep into a large crack formed in the desktop by Tonglong's powerful blow. That impact would have easily cracked bone.

"*Sign it*," Tonglong said again, his voice as tight as an archer's bow.

"I will not," the Emperor replied indignantly. "You are asking me to grant you the freedom to forcibly recruit every male in the entire country between the ages of eight and fifty into your army. I cannot allow this. We are not at war."

"You can, and you will," Tonglong said. "Emperors have been conscripting people into military service for thousands of years, and not just for war. Do you not remember how the Great Wall was built?"

"In this case it is not justified."

"The only justification you need is that I say it shall be so," Tonglong said. "I will say this only one more time. Sign it."

"I repeat: I will not. What can you do?"

Tonglong reached out with amazing speed and grabbed the Emperor's left thumb. With a powerful yank, he wrenched the thumb in a complete circle. ShaoShu shuddered as the sound of crunching bone mixed with the Emperor's startled scream.

Tonglong released his grip and growled, "There are at least two hundred more bones in your body. Would you like to pick the next one? Or should I?"

The Emperor struggled to regain his composure, tucking his mangled hand into his lap. In a shaky voice, he said, "I will sign it."

"That's a good puppet," Tonglong said, dipping a writing brush into the spilled ink. He spread out one of the scattered scrolls, and the Emperor signed it.

"Now seal it," Tonglong said.

The Emperor reached into the folds of the rough robe that he now wore in place of his fine silk garments, and he pulled out a small clay pendant hanging from a cord around his neck.

"I wondered what that was," Tonglong said. "I assumed it was a simple dragon pendant. I should have known better."

The Emperor did not reply. Instead, he held the small rectangular object before him in his good hand and awkwardly untied a knot that had been positioned very close to one edge. The pendant separated into two halves. The back half was plain and smooth on all of its surfaces. The front half, however, was different. A simple dragon had been carved on the outside to make it look like a standard pendant, but an elaborate dragon had been painstakingly carved on the inside portion.

Tonglong snatched the seal from the Emperor's hand and dipped the special dragon into the spilled ink. Then he pressed the seal against the decree, below the Emperor's signature.

ShaoShu watched Tonglong apply a steady, even pressure in order to make the seal stand out clearly, and something unexpected happened. The seal crumbled to dust between Tonglong's fingers.

Tonglong hissed and reached across his desk with one hand, grabbing the Emperor by the throat. "How dare you play games with me!"

"No games," the Emperor somehow managed to say. "It may still have worked. Look closely."

ShaoShu looked at the paper from across the room, but all he saw was a blob of black ink and clay powder.

Tonglong took the paper in his free hand and tilted it sideways, shaking it. The powder drifted from the decree, and ShaoShu saw that the seal was somewhat smeared but still identifiable, even from a distance. He did not know a thing about official documents, but this one looked authentic to him.

Tonglong released the Emperor's throat. "It was designed to disintegrate like that, wasn't it?"

The Emperor nodded and coughed. "It is a safeguard against unauthorized use. It is meant to break and destroy the seal's mark as well. You must have an extraordinarily soft touch."

"We will see how soft my touch is when I start breaking more of your fingers. Where are the real seals?"

"That seal was real."

"I mean, where are the ones you use on a regular basis? I doubt you use those clay versions."

"The royal set is back at the Forbidden City, in Peking."

"Do you have more clay seals?"

"No."

Tonglong stood and pounded his fist on the desk again. He glared at the Emperor. "You know what this means, don't you?"

"It means that you will have to keep me alive longer than you expected. You will never be able to execute another initiative like this conscription without the seals, and you will not be allowed inside the Forbidden City without me."

"Plenty of new emperors have entered the Forbidden City with the old Emperor's head on a spike."

"But not you," the Emperor challenged. "At least, not yet. You still have the substantial Western army to contend with. From what I have overheard among your men, Xie is alive and well. If he makes it back to his homeland, he will take the role his father held as Western Warlord, and his people will crush you. They are a powerful, merciless lot. And they have horses. There are also the imperial forces under my direct supervision within the walls of the Forbidden City."

"Your Forbidden City forces are more susceptible than you think," Tonglong jeered. "A little bit of treasure and the promise of power have gone a long way right beneath your nose."

"My men are loyal to the death."

Tonglong laughed. "Why? Because you pay them well? I will pay them more. In fact, I already have. I have one key individual who has made me confident that I will win the rest over soon enough. He will convince the others to join—or kill them. With your own imperial forces turned against you, combined with my current Southern and Eastern armies and the men I will recruit, even the mighty Western army will not stand a chance."

"Do not forget about the bandits and their Resistance," the Emperor said. "They will declare all-out war against someone like you. They have been a thorn in my side for years."

"Let them try. I crushed them once and took their stronghold, and I will gladly do it again. Their life span is coming to an end. As for *your* life span, you are correct. You will walk this earth at least a little longer. Signatures are easy enough to forge, but that seal is far too complicated to reproduce without an original to copy. If you cooperate, I *may* let you live once we reach the Forbidden City."

Tonglong picked up the decree and stared at the seal, shaking his head. He carried the document to the far side of the room and placed it on top of a long table, then glanced at the mess he had made on the desk and the scrolls he had knocked to the floor. "ShaoShu, tidy up this place. I am taking the Emperor back to his private pigsty now."

ShaoShu swallowed hard. "Yes, sir."

Tonglong headed for the door, and ShaoShu hurriedly unlocked it, holding it open. Tonglong passed through it with the Emperor in tow, and ShaoShu risked giving the Emperor a quick wink. The Emperor nodded slightly, as though he understood that he and ShaoShu were on the same side, and ShaoShu locked the door again.

ShaoShu hurried over to the desk area, scooping up a handful of scrolls from the floor. He tried to open the desk's topmost drawer, but it was locked. He tried a second drawer, and this one slid smoothly open. It was empty, and he managed to carefully place half of the scrolls into it before it was full. He found another empty drawer and set the remaining scrolls in it. He had begun to walk away to find some rags to wipe up the spilled ink and powder when curiosity got the better of him.

He walked back to the desk and checked the remaining drawers. All were unlocked, and most were empty. Those that were not empty contained things you would expect to find in a desk—blank scrolls, ink, writing brushes, writing quills.

ShaoShu tugged at the desk's only locked drawer again, wondering what might be hidden inside. Maybe it was something that could help Long and the others? Having lived alone on the streets most of his life, ShaoShu had developed skills to help him survive. One of those skills was picking locks.

He reopened a drawer containing writing quills and selected the largest, most rigid one. The end had already been sharpened to a thin point, and he stuck the point into the desk drawer's lock. After a few careful pokes and a turn of his wrist, ShaoShu gave the quill a gentle push and the lock disengaged.

He pulled the drawer open to find more scrolls. Two of them looked very old and battered, and he couldn't help taking a peek. While he could not read, he recognized immediately what they were. Alongside the words he saw detailed sketches of people standing in complex body positions combined with different movement sequences. All of the people had their hands held out in front of them like dragon claws. One of the scrolls even included a series with weapons. It depicted a figure with a sword in one hand and a chain whip in the other.

These were some of the dragon scrolls from the destroyed Cangzhen Temple. Ying had been after them, and ShaoShu recalled Ying once telling him how Tonglong had managed to steal several right out from under his nose.

ShaoShu grinned and slipped both scrolls into the folds of his robe. Maybe they would prove useful to his friends.

CHAPTER 7

Over the next week, Long's condition improved noticeably, but not as much as Hok would have liked. While he could sit up on his own now and go a full day without drifting off into an exhausted slumber, he was still unable to stand. He blamed it on the tumultuous seas and rough weather. Hok blamed it on her herb bag.

Hok was able to make him blood-enriching tonics and infection-inhibiting ointments, and he did benefit greatly from vast quantities of sleep and the nutritious food Charles had stowed aboard. However, Hok said that she lacked a few rare items that she was certain would speed his recovery even more. She had hoped to make a stop along the way to pick up the necessary ingredients, but Charles would not allow it. He was justifiably concerned that Tonglong might have already spread word overland that they were to be captured on sight. Additionally, the winds had not been favorable for docking in any of the ports they had passed. While it would have been easy to sail into any one of them, the prevailing winds would have prevented them from sailing back out. Moreover, once they had left the sea and begun to head up the Yellow River, Charles' determination to stay away from the waterside towns had only grown stronger.

Hok had to settle for the next best thing, which was stopping somewhere both she and Charles knew to be safe that also had the supplies Hok wanted. She knew the perfect place: the home of an elderly healer called PawPaw, or Grandmother. It was along their route to the Jade Phoenix in the city of Kaifeng, and from Charles' estimation they would arrive very soon.

As Charles' sloop cut a smooth swath up the Yellow River's fast-moving current, Long sat with his back against the boat's side rail. Like the others, he spent most of his time scanning the area for trouble. There was plenty of scenery but very few people, and consequently no conflicts. Steep banks of yellow earth shouldered both sides of the river in this region, covered with a matting of dead grass and dried, broken reed stalks. The trees were nearly leafless, their skeleton frames shaking in the chilly breeze. Fortunately, Charles had several blankets in his sea chest to keep them all warm. They would have to acquire jackets, boots, hats, and gloves once they reached Kaifeng. They were now in the north, after all, and snow was not unheard of this time of year.

They rounded a bend in the river, and Charles pointed to the shore. "There it is," he said, his finger aimed at a small house perched atop the riverbank. "It looks different now that the leaves have fallen."

"It sure does," Hok said. "I see smoke drifting from the chimney, though. It seems someone is home."

"That's g-g-great," Malao stammered from the mast top, his teeth chattering. "I c-c-can't wait to warm up!" He quickly untied a few ropes and coiled them up, then scurried down the mast, onto the deck, stopping next to Charles. "All c-c-clear, C-C-Captain."

"Thanks, Malao," Charles said, looking up at the mast top. "I couldn't have done better myself. Can you give me a hand with the mainsail?"

"S-s-sure," Malao replied.

Charles nodded and turned to Hok and Xie. "When the big sail starts to come down, could you two do your best to grab it?"

"Of course," they replied.

"Very good," Charles said. He turned to Fu in the bow. "Are you ready?"

"Aye, Captain," Fu said, and he gripped the head of a large anchor.

"On my mark, then," Charles said. "Ready . . . and . . . anchor away!"

Fu heaved the heavy anchor overboard with a loud grunt, and Long watched as Malao and Charles began to pull furiously on a complicated series of ropes attached to the mast. The sloop's mainsail dropped like a billowing cloud, and Hok and Xie scrambled about the deck, doing their best to scoop it into their arms before it slipped into the water.

"Hang on!" Fu warned.

Long turned to watch the anchor's thick rope playing out quickly through Fu's hands over the side of the sloop. The rope slackened for an instant, and Fu hurriedly wound it around a cleat. An instant later, the rope went taut and the boat stopped its forward progress with a violent jerk. The sloop then began to drift backward with the current until the rope went taut again, the boat stopping altogether with its nose still facing upstream.

"Well done, everyone," Charles said as he glanced around the boat. He began to untie his robe sash, and Long asked, "What are you doing?"

"Someone is going to have to get wet," Charles said. "It might as well be the captain."

Charles slipped off his robe, and Long saw for the first time that he had a pair of matching pistols in holsters strapped across his pale chest. Charles removed the pistols and holsters, as well as his boots.

"Malao, the bow rope, please," Charles said.

Malao handed Charles a section of sturdy rope, and Charles placed it between his teeth. He grinned, nodded to the group, and dove overboard.

Long watched as Charles surfaced in the muddy water with a loud gasp, the frigid temperature doubtless a shock to his system. He did not complain, though, and swam powerfully to shore before scrambling up the riverbank. Once he reached the top, he took the end of the rope from his teeth and tied it to a thick tree trunk, then waved.

Long was surprised to feel the boat begin to move. He glanced toward the bow and saw Fu pulling the opposite end of the rope, his face red with exertion.

"Use the winch, Fu!" Charles called out, but Fu ignored him. Instead, Fu continued to heave on the rope hand over hand until the boat's keel scraped the river's bottom close to shore. Fu stopped heaving and tied the rope off.

"Well done, you stubborn pussycat," Charles called out. "A winch would have made for a lot less effort. Malao, toss me the stern line!"

Malao did not obey, either. Instead, he threw a coil of rope over his shoulder, jumped onto the boat's side rail, and made a tremendous leap ashore. He landed well clear of the water and played out rope as he raced up the bank, handing the coil to Charles.

"Show-offs," Charles said, shivering in the cold breeze. "You did remember to tie the other end of this line to a cleat, right?"

Malao giggled. "Of course."

Charles tied the stern line to a second tree trunk, and he slid back down the bank through the yellow mud. Long watched him step back into the water and wade over to the sloop, the water reaching above his waist.

"Xie," Charles said, shivering more violently now. "Help Long down onto my shoulders."

Long wanted to protest, but knew there would be no point. He allowed Xie to lower his legs onto Charles' cold, wet shoulders, and Charles quickly waded to shore, depositing Long on solid ground. Malao helped Long up the bank, and when they reached the top, Long looked back to see Hok and Xie leap directly onto the shore as Malao had done.

Hok hurried over to Charles and wrapped him in a blanket she'd brought, while Xie held up a bundle. It was another blanket wrapped around Charles' pistols and holsters. Xie unwrapped the blanket, draped it over Charles' head, and said, "I will hang on to your firearms until you have warmed up."

"Th-th-thank you," Charles stammered, his lips beginning to turn purple.

Long felt his *dan tien* begin to tingle, and he turned toward the house. A hunched figure in a hooded overcoat appeared from the opposite side of the structure, and an elderly female voice called out, "Why, Charles! Your sloop looks very different! I hardly recognized it from my window. Come in and dry off. Hok, Malao, Fu! So good to see you. Bring your friends and get yourselves out of this vile cold weather."

The woman headed back the way she had come and disappeared, and the others hurried after her. Malao led the charge toward the house, followed by Hok and Fu with Charles between them. Long and Xie brought up the rear.

As they approached the home, Long took in the details. The house was small and old, but still in good condition. Most of the window shutters had been nailed shut for the winter, and the heavy front door appeared to have been designed to keep out more than the cold. It also looked like it had been broken down and repaired several times. As he entered the house and closed the door behind him, the old woman saw him eyeballing the pockmarked doorjamb.

"Occasionally, I receive unwelcome or impatient visitors," she said with a smile. "You, however, will be received like family. Welcome. I am PawPaw."

Long bowed. "I am Long. Thank you for allowing me into your home."

Xie bowed, too. "I am Xie. I thank you as well."

"No need for bows, and certainly no need for thank-yous," PawPaw said, throwing back her hood to reveal thin gray hair and clear, sharp eyes. "I have not done anything. My home is your home. Tell me, what happened to your leg, Long? I noticed you limping and I can see the lump of a bandage on your thigh. There is one on your left arm, too."

"It is a long story," Long replied, unsure how much information he should share. He glanced at Hok.

"It's okay," Hok said, pointing to the front door. "PawPaw will understand our predicament better than anyone. She is an ally of the bandits, and is a key link in their information chain. That is how her door got that way."

PawPaw smiled warmly, and Long found himself

smiling back. "I see," he said. "In that case, I was sliced open by a man with a hidden dagger in the Shanghai Fight Club pit arena, then chased by soldiers under the leadership of a man called Tonglong. Hok sewed me back together. Do you know who Tonglong is?"

PawPaw nodded. "I do. Are you poor dears running from him?"

"Yes," Hok replied. "That is why Charles' sloop looks different. He changed its appearance to fool Tonglong. We are in trouble and need to see the bandits as soon as possible."

PawPaw looked at Long's leg. "All of you?"

"No," Hok said. "If you do not mind, we would like my temple brother Long to stay here with you. He needs to heal."

"Excuse me?" Long said. "You aren't going anywhere without me."

Xie laid a firm hand on Long's shoulder. "Yes, we are. Hok and I have already discussed this, and you have no say in the matter. If it is agreeable with PawPaw, you will remain here while Charles takes the rest of us to Kaifeng in his boat. Once there, Hok, Malao, and Fu will seek out the bandits, while I continue home alone. Charles will head off on his own, too, traveling back to the southern sea in search of the pirates. He will attempt to obtain firearms for us."

Long frowned.

"You are in no condition to travel overland," Hok said. "Your stitches need to come out in the next day or two, and afterward you must not put too much strain on your leg or arm. Walking the distances we must travel would be too much for you right now. Once you have healed, of course we would like you to join us with Mong and the bandits. By the time you reach us, we will hopefully have a plan to deal with Tonglong. Someone will then need to share that plan with Xie, and the most likely candidate is you."

Long looked at Xie.

Xie nodded. "That is right. It is a long and treacherous journey to the city of Tunhuang—my homeland. However, an individual can do the trip relatively quickly, provided he or she has the right equipment. Have you ever ridden a horse?"

"No," Long said.

"Then you will have to learn," Xie said. "I have a contact in Kaifeng who breeds horses unlike any other in China. I will take one of his mounts for my journey home, and I will make arrangements for you to have one as well. You must heal first, though. You cannot ride with your leg in that condition."

PawPaw looked at Xie. "You are the son of the Western Warlord, are you not?"

Xie's eyebrows rose. "I am. How did you know?"

"I make it my business to know things," PawPaw said. "I recently received important news from a black market dealer in Jinan called HukJee—Black Pig. He has received reports from within Tonglong's ranks that Tonglong has slain his own mother, as well as your father. I am sorry."

Long saw Xie's massive jaw muscles tighten. "Bad news travels quickly," Xie said.

"It does," PawPaw replied. "And there is more. Tonglong's people are spreading the claim that he had no choice but to take action against your father because your father was planning to revolt against the Emperor. They also say that you escaped from Tonglong with the help of a fight club fighter called Golden Dragon, and that you intend to carry out your father's plan. Tonglong says that the Emperor is in his protective custody because of this threat to national security, and he is currently assembling an army of civilians to join his existing troops and march upon your lands."

Xie scowled. "The lying dog! I must get back to my people." He turned to Charles, who was crouched next to PawPaw's fireplace. "How long do you think it will be before we can leave?"

"Give me half an hour and a bowl of hot soup," Charles said, "and I'll be ready."

PawPaw smiled. "I will get the soup started."

"Thank you," Xie said. "All of you. Your kindness will not be forgotten." He removed a large ring from his little finger and handed it to Long. It was a jade scorpion resting atop a small mountain of gold.

Long slipped the ring onto his thumb.

"After you have healed," Xie said, "go to Kaifeng and seek out a horseman called Cang. He is quite famous and will not be difficult to find. Show him this ring. He will take care of the rest. Any questions?"

"I suppose I have one," Long said. "Should I really do this on my own?"

"Unfortunately, yes. It will be asking a great deal for Cang to provide me with a horse, as well as you. Asking for a third might be out of the question."

"Can someone ride the horse with me?"

"No. The journey is too taxing to expect a horse to carry more than one rider."

Long nodded.

PawPaw glanced at Hok. "How long do you think it will be before Long has healed enough to handle the stress of riding a horse for several days?"

"I would estimate four weeks," Hok replied. "That is, if you have a complete stock of healing herbs. He could probably sit on a horse for short periods in about two weeks, which is what I would consider to be the time frame for a general recovery. Is that acceptable?"

"Of course," PawPaw replied. "I am just trying to make plans of my own. Do you know how to find Mong once you reach Kaifeng?"

"Yes," Hok said. "We need to talk with Yuen at the Jade Phoenix."

"Perfect," PawPaw said. "She can tell you how to find them. The bandits are constantly on the move. Even so, it should take you less than a week to reach them. They live in the forest, but tend to remain relatively close to Kaifeng. As soon as you arrive, ask Mong to send three strong men to me with two horse carts. By the time we load up and return to the bandits' camp, and Long travels to Kaifeng, his leg should be healed."

"We?" Hok asked.

"I am going to the bandit camp, too," PawPaw said. "There is war on the horizon. Mong is going to need all the help he can get."

CHAPTER 8

ShaoShu sat on the edge of his bed, picking lint out of his belly button. He had not been this bored in a very long time.

Since the incident with the Emperor and the spilled ink several days ago, he had been kept away from Tonglong's command center office and meeting rooms. In fact, he had been excluded from just about everything, spending nearly all of his time in this makeshift bedroom. Tonglong had recruited a group of elite soldiers to follow him around to do his bidding, and one of these soldiers had caught ShaoShu trying to sneak extra food to the Emperor. Consequently, he had been confined here.

This was just as well, as far as ShaoShu was concerned. The more distance between him and Tonglong, the better. He had heard a few things about what the sneaky mantis was up to, and he did not like any of it. For example, just that morning he'd overheard a conversation about Tonglong showering his elite soldiers with money to keep hidden the fact that the Emperor was currently being held prisoner in the pig crate. Everyone knew that the Emperor was with Tonglong, but they thought that he was being luxuriously catered to in one of the wings of this massive building.

ShaoShu had also heard that Tonglong was sending vast sums of money to the Forbidden City to bribe people to do his bidding. This money was said to be coming from the sale of some of the treasure Tonglong had stolen from Ying's family, and this upset ShaoShu. However, there was little that he could do about it. He could not just sneak away and find Ying to tell him about it. Not only did he not know where Ying was, there was always one of those elite soldiers near his door. He had tried to sneak out before, but never had any luck.

ShaoShu pouted. He hated being stuck in this room.

A pouch tied to his sash began to wriggle, and ShaoShu looked down to see his pet mouse poke its head out of the soft bag. It was probably hungry. He had taken the mouse into his care while he was stowed away on a boat Tonglong had commandeered. This was before Tonglong had even become the Southern Warlord. Until now, keeping his pet happy and fed regularly had not been a problem.

"I'm sorry, little one," ShaoShu said, taking the

mouse out and stroking its head. "I can't just go and swipe food for us whenever I like, like I used to. I have to wait for it to be delivered. I don't even get to pick what we eat. I know the things they have been bringing lately are no good for mice. I'm sorry."

The mouse looked up at him with sad eyes, and ShaoShu scratched its scrawny sides, running his fingers along its protruding ribs.

"Maybe I should let you go?" ShaoShu said. "You can go places I can't. You would probably be better off free. I'll let you decide."

ShaoShu placed the mouse on the floor. It stood still for a moment, staring at him; then it twitched its nose and scurried away beneath the door.

ShaoShu sighed. "Goodbye, my friend."

He wished he could do the same thing. He was very good at squeezing through tight spaces, but he had not been able to figure out a way to escape this place. Tonglong's elite soldiers were the best of the best, and as good as he was at creeping around, he could not sneak past them. He would be stuck here forever.

Unless—

Unless he just made a break for it. Forgot stealth and simply ran. After all, he was small, quick, and nimble. It might be worth a try. Besides, he would go crazy otherwise, just sitting in this room all day and night.

ShaoShu decided to give it a try. He crossed the room, checked to make sure the two dragon scrolls he had swiped were securely hidden deep within the folds of his robe, and slowly pulled his door open.

He got lucky. There was a soldier looming nearby as always, and this man was very close—only two paces away. Perfect. Before the soldier could even open his mouth to ask what he was doing, ShaoShu lowered his head and ran right between the man's legs. The soldier snatched at him, but missed. As the man spun around to begin his pursuit, ShaoShu picked up speed.

"Stop, you little rodent!" the soldier yelled.

ShaoShu didn't look back. He saw that this corridor was coming to an end ahead, and he had to make a decision: turn right or left. He chose left.

He should have chosen right.

As ShaoShu rounded the corner, he crashed head-first into Tonglong, who was striding forward. ShaoShu spun to one side in an effort to get around Tonglong, but Tonglong's hand snapped downward with incredible speed and latched on to the back of ShaoShu's neck. ShaoShu squealed in pain, and Tonglong responded by squeezing even harder. Tonglong's grip was amazing.

ShaoShu began to sob. "Please stop, sir. That really hurts."

A group of elite soldiers rushed forward from behind Tonglong, and the disgraced soldier that ShaoShu had evaded approached from the opposite direction. Once ShaoShu and Tonglong were surrounded, Tonglong released his grip, shoving ShaoShu's face toward the floor.

"*Kowtow,*" Tonglong said.

ShaoShu obeyed. He dropped to his knees and tapped his forehead against the floor three times before focusing his eyes on the tops of Tonglong's heavy boots.

"Rise," Tonglong said.

ShaoShu stood.

"Where do you think you are going?" Tonglong asked.

ShaoShu shrugged. "Nowhere, sir."

"That is right," Tonglong said. "Did you honestly think you could get out of here?"

Knowing that Tonglong appreciated strong individuals, ShaoShu lifted his head and pointed at the disgraced soldier. "I got past him."

ShaoShu braced himself for a blow from Tonglong, but it never came. Instead, Tonglong laughed.

"I suppose you are right, Little Mouse. How quickly I forget your particular abilities." Tonglong looked at the disgraced soldier. "Get out of my sight. I will deal with you later."

"Yes, sir!" the soldier replied, and hurried away.

Tonglong spoke to ShaoShu once more. "I seem to have been ignoring you these past several days. I imagine you are getting bored sitting alone in that room all day long."

"Yes, sir," ShaoShu said.

"I can fix that. Come with me."

ShaoShu stood and followed Tonglong into his command center office. Tonglong told him to have a seat in front of the large desk, and then he ordered his men to wait outside the room. The soldiers left and closed the door behind them, and Tonglong sat down opposite ShaoShu, pulling a small blank scroll, a writing quill, and some ink out of a drawer.

"Do you think you can find the Shanghai Fight Club?" Tonglong asked.

"Yes, sir," ShaoShu said. "It's only a few *li* from here. I remember coming straight to this place after the Fight Club Championship."

"Good," Tonglong said. "I would like you to deliver a message to the fight club owner. It is something I do not want anyone else to know, and I think you are the perfect person to deliver it."

ShaoShu pouted. "Because I can't read, sir?"

"That is right," Tonglong said. "Because you cannot read."

Tonglong wrote a single line on the scroll and took a small handful of sand from an ornate container on the desk. He sprinkled the sand over the newly written characters, dusted it off, and checked the ink with his finger. It was dry. He rolled up the scroll and handed it to ShaoShu.

"The fight club owner's name is Yang. Give this to him and come straight back here." Tonglong reached into a pouch tied to his sash and pulled out a large gold coin. "This will be yours when you return."

ShaoShu stared at the coin in disbelief. Shiny objects had always fascinated him, and this was the shiniest thing he had ever seen. Rays of light bounced off it from sunbeams coming in through Tonglong's unshuttered window. Besides being shiny, that single coin was worth a small fortune.

"I reward those who are loyal to me," Tonglong said, adjusting his long ponytail braid. His robe slipped open slightly, and ShaoShu could not help but notice another shiny object, the key Tonglong wore around his neck. It was the same one that ShaoShu had removed from Tonglong's father's tomb. It looked different from any key he had ever seen, and was entwined with dragons. Tonglong claimed it was the key to the Forbidden City.

Tonglong pulled his robe closed. "I see the memory of my father's tomb is still fresh in your mind. I will be putting the key to use soon enough. It would be wise for you to not talk about it with anyone. Ever."

"No, sir," ShaoShu said, growing nervous.

"Good boy," Tonglong replied. "Now run along. If you complete this assignment before dark, I will give you *two* gold coins."

ShaoShu's eyes lit up, and he jumped out of his chair. He would love to have two gold coins that size, but he knew that was never going to happen. As soon as he was clear of this command center, he would head in the opposite direction from the fight club and never stop running until he found Ying or Long. He had had enough of Tonglong.

Tonglong ordered his men to open the office door, and as ShaoShu scurried through it, Tonglong gave the men clear instructions to leave ShaoShu alone. He was departing on a special mission.

The soldiers complied.

ShaoShu hurried outside and was immediately

struck by how cold it was, even with the sun out. Winter was definitely close. He would have gone back inside to get an overcoat, but realized that he did not have one. This was going to make his escape more difficult, or at least more uncomfortable.

He decided to jog in order to both keep himself warm and get away from Tonglong faster. He had only gone two blocks and was still within sight of Tonglong's command center when someone began to shout.

"Hey! Kid! You, there! STOP, IN THE NAME OF THE LAW!"

Huh? ShaoShu thought, and he saw a very old man hobble into the road ahead of him. The old man wore a shopkeeper's apron, and he began to wave his arms frantically.

ShaoShu frowned and slowed to a walk. As he neared the old man, the same voice called out, "Stop, I said!"

Confused, ShaoShu looked around and realized that the voice did not belong to the shopkeeper in the road. Instead, it belonged to an ancient butcher whose store was located across the street from the shopkeeper. The butcher stepped out from behind his meat counter and waved a large cleaver.

ShaoShu stopped dead in his tracks. Behind him, he heard someone else shout, "Keep him there, old-timers! We're coming!"

ShaoShu turned to see a group of seven soldiers running toward him from the direction of Tonglong's command center. ShaoShu did not recognize any of these men, however. They were not wearing the red uniforms of Tonglong's elite team. What was going on? The soldiers ran up to him, and two of them grabbed his arms while a third gripped the back of his robe.

"Nice work," the soldier gripping his robe said to the shopkeeper. "I will deliver your reward as soon as I process the paperwork."

"*His* reward!" the butcher said. "I saw him first! Didn't you hear me shout?"

"No, *I* saw him first," the shopkeeper argued angrily. "The bounty is mine!"

"There will be time to sort this out later, you two," the soldier said. "Haven't you both collected enough bounties already? I am not even sure this kid qualifies. He might be too young."

"He is plenty old enough," one of the old men said. "Pay up."

"What is happening?" ShaoShu asked. "Why are you doing this? What bounty are you talking about?"

"Do not play dumb with me, kid," the soldier said. "We have been recruiting every man and boy for Warlord Tonglong's army for days now. I do not know how you managed to hide from us all this time, but it looks like you are in the army now."

ShaoShu remembered the scroll Tonglong had made the Emperor sign. That must be what this was all about. "You mean you're just going to take me straight off to the army?" he asked. "Without telling anyone? What about my, um, family?"

"When you do not come home, they will know exactly what happened," the soldier said. "Everyone is accustomed to it by now. Every man and boy in the entire region is being fitted for a uniform at this moment. Now come with us. We need to find a way to verify your age."

"You had better let me go!" ShaoShu warned, growing angry. How could Tonglong do this? "Listen," he said. "Southern Warlord Tonglong has sent me out to deliver an important message to the owner of the Shanghai Fight Club. If you don't believe me, just ask him."

The soldier laughed. "You don't say? Can I take a look at this message of yours?"

"No," ShaoShu said. "It's secret."

"I will see about that," the soldier replied, reaching into the folds of ShaoShu's robe. ShaoShu wriggled and squirmed, but the man still managed to grab hold of the small scroll and pull it out. Fortunately, the dragon scrolls remained hidden.

The soldier unrolled the scroll, and his eyes narrowed. "Is this your idea of a joke?"

"No," ShaoShu said. "Why?"

"Because of what it says, you little runt. You are going to pay for this!"

"How am I supposed to know what it says?" ShaoShu asked. "I can't even read!"

The soldier's eyes narrowed even more. "It says, 'Major Guan is a buffoon.'"

"Who is Major Guan?"

"Me!" the soldier roared. "I am in charge of rounding up all the dodgers—people like you who try to hide from their responsibility to answer the Emperor's call for additional troops. As if you did not already know this. Tie him up!"

"Wait—" ShaoShu began, but his words were cut off by his head being shoved forward until his chin dug into his chest. One soldier kept his head pinned in that position while another soldier yanked his arms behind his back. A third soldier crossed ShaoShu's wrists and began to tie them together with a rough cord.

ShaoShu did not despair. His life on the streets had put him in the path of constables before, and he had been through this routine more times than he would like to admit. He knew just what to do.

He made fists with both hands, tensing his forearm muscles as the unseen soldier wound the cord around his wrists, behind his back. ShaoShu pressed his flexed forearms outward against the cord with steadily increasing pressure until his wrists ached. He maintained the pressure even after the man had finished.

ShaoShu's head was released, and he lifted it up. Behind his back he felt the cool breeze blowing through the open space he had managed to leave between his wrists, and he forced down a smile.

"This way," Major Guan growled, and the six other soldiers replied, "Yes, sir!"

One of the soldiers gave ShaoShu a shove, and they began marching toward the compound. The men surrounded ShaoShu as they walked, but they kept their hands off him.

That was their first mistake.

Their second mistake came when a pretty young girl stepped into the road behind them and approached the old shopkeeper. All the soldiers turned to look at her.

ShaoShu took advantage of the distraction. He pressed his wrists together to close the gap he had left between them and unclenched his fists, straightening his fingers. He quickly folded his right palm upon itself by touching the tip of his thumb to the tip of his little finger, and slid his uncommonly flexible folded right hand out from beneath the bindings in one smooth motion.

His hands were free. ShaoShu balled them into fists, and as Major Guan turned to face him to continue walking, ShaoShu drove them both straight into the major's groin.

Major Guan cried out and hunched forward, and ShaoShu zipped around him, racing away from the command center. He had taken only a few steps when he heard pistol shots and the sound of horses' hooves. ShaoShu turned to see Tonglong and several soldiers racing down the road toward him atop squat, hairy stallions.

ShaoShu knew better than to try to run any farther. He stopped, and Tonglong was beside him a moment later.

"Going somewhere?" Tonglong asked.

ShaoShu was scared, but he was also angry. Tonglong had set him up with that note. He knew that ShaoShu was going to get nabbed as soon as he set foot on the street. ShaoShu found that he could not contain himself. "You knew I would get caught, didn't you?"

"Yes," Tonglong replied with a smirk. "But I also had a hunch that you would escape. And I was right."

"It was a test?"

"Yes, and you passed with flying colors, unfortunately." Tonglong pulled two gold coins from the pouch on his sash and threw them to ShaoShu. "You have earned those, Little Mouse. You managed to find a flaw in my recruitment enforcers' procedures. I will have to fix that, beginning with the proper way to tie knots." He nodded to the bundle of cord still hanging from ShaoShu's left wrist.

ShaoShu stared at Tonglong. "What if I had failed?"

"Then you would likely begin training as a powder boy first thing tomorrow morning. We can always use fast, nimble children like you on the battlefield to carry cannon fuses and other items to the front lines."

ShaoShu looked away from Tonglong, frustrated.

"Cheer up, ShaoShu," Tonglong said. "You succeeded, which means you will remain with me. I will even have a red uniform made for you so that no one will question you again."

"Thank you, sir," ShaoShu mumbled, still unable to look at Tonglong. He glanced at Tonglong's horse.

Tonglong patted the animal's neck. "You did not know that I am a horseman, did you? I have been riding all my life, and I have the finest stallion in China waiting for me at a former bandit stronghold. I have not seen him in several months. This stubby, hairy one will have to do for now."

ShaoShu glanced at Tonglong, and Tonglong pointed at the gold coins in ShaoShu's hand. "We are packing up and moving out tomorrow. I suggest you exchange some of your new wealth for a means of transportation. I will have one of my elite men take you pony shopping today. It is a long walk to the Forbidden City."

CHAPTER 9

It had taken Long and PawPaw nearly two weeks to pack up all of PawPaw's belongings, and he was glad to be almost finished with the task. She did not have much in the way of clothes or furniture, but he guessed that she had more medicinal herbs than the best apothecary shops in the largest of cities. Many of the items were rather odd, and she seemed to have saved the strangest for last.

"What are these?" Long asked, holding up a stack of thin, rigid black wafers, each roughly the same size as his palm.

"Dried fruit bats," PawPaw replied. "Good for digestion."

"What about these?" he said, poking a finger into a small container of tiny dried objects.

"Don't touch those!" PawPaw snapped. "Larks' tongues. Very expensive."

Long pulled his finger away and shrugged. He wrapped these final fragile items and moved on to the remaining bulky objects, like dried deer antlers and whole tortoiseshells that would one day be ground into powder.

Thanks to PawPaw's constant attention, Long's health had steadily improved and he could now handle nearly any task she threw at him. She had removed his stitches, and both wounds were healing nicely. Hok's estimate of a two-week general recovery proved to be accurate, and he was healthy enough to travel. He was probably even ready to climb onto a horse.

Horses had been on Long's mind ever since Xie had first mentioned them, and Long was somewhat relieved when the bandit escorts finally arrived with two workhorses, each pulling an empty cart. It meant that he would get a chance to observe the animals up close before he would ever have to climb onto one's back. In some ways, he wished that he could observe the bandits in advance, too.

His sensitive *dan tien* had detected the bandits approaching well before they knocked on PawPaw's door, and he was not sure he liked what he saw. Peering out of PawPaw's shuttered windows, Long saw the first bandit come into view, and he was one of the strangest-looking humans Long had ever seen. The man had a stubby torso, curiously long arms, and a ratty mustache that reached all the way down to his chest. He was filthy, and even from a distance Long could see that his nose was very wide and almost completely flat. Thick scar tissue crisscrossed his forehead and cheeks, a clear sign that the man was a veteran fighter. He must be NgGung—Centipede.

Hok and the others had told him about NgGung. They had said that he was a very nice man, but warned that he loved to play a game called "One new thing you'll know for every blow." Apparently, NgGung would encourage people he had just met to fight him as a means of exchanging information.

Fortunately, PawPaw was familiar with NgGung's ways. She hurried outside to greet him alone, while Long continued to peer through the shutters, sizing up the other two bandits. One was a thick but pleasant-looking man with a clean-shaven head and face. He looked a surprising amount like Fu, and was surely Fu's father, Sanfu—Mountain Tiger.

The other man was gargantuan, with short, greasy hair and the heaviest beard Long had ever seen. He had to be Hung, or Bear. Malao had told Long about a fight he'd had with Hung many months ago, and Long made a mental note to not get on Hung's bad side.

PawPaw called Long outside to meet the group, and, thankfully, NgGung made no mention of his crazy game. After a few formalities, they got right to loading PawPaw's things into the carts.

Hung made it clear from the beginning that he was in charge, and that they were in a hurry. It was midmorning, and he hoped to be on the way by mid-afternoon. PawPaw encouraged him and the others to spend a restful night at her home instead and head out first thing the following morning, but Hung would not hear of it. He said that he was eager to return to their camp as soon as possible, because they had received reports that Tonglong and his army were heading in their direction. They had a lot of work to do to prepare for what he felt would be an unavoidable battle.

Long worked quickly and silently alongside the bandits, and they finished faster than Long would have believed possible. The men were careful and efficient. He was impressed.

Hung's plan was to travel until dark unless there was a bright moon, in which case they would march for as long as possible by its light, too. It had taken the bandits six days to get there, and even though the carts were now fully weighted down, Hung wanted to return in five. He allowed them to quickly eat a hot meal Paw-Paw had prepared, and they left.

Long fell into stride beside NgGung at the head of the caravan, leading the first horse with its cart. Sanfu took up a position at the center of the group, leading the second horse and cart with PawPaw riding atop it. Hung guarded their flank, his gigantic war hammers at his side.

Long and NgGung talked for hours as they walked. Despite NgGung's rough outward appearance, Long found him to be very interesting and intelligent. As one of the bandits' main spies, NgGung knew a great deal about the politics of the region. He and Long discussed everything from Tonglong to the Emperor to Cangzhen Temple.

Long learned that many of the bandits were once monks who lived at Cangzhen. They had left over a disagreement with Grandmaster years ago, but they still held a great respect for him and his memory. In their opinion, Grandmaster had gotten overly involved in politics, especially where the current Emperor was concerned. The bandits disliked the Emperor, but they believed that things would be much worse if Tonglong took control of the throne. They vowed to stop him at any cost.

It was dusk before Long and NgGung's conversation started to dwindle. At this time, Long began to pay more attention to the forest sounds around him, and he could have sworn the noise level was diminishing. He soon felt his *dan tien* begin to warm, and he turned to NgGung. "Something is not right."

NgGung nodded and raised a hand to stop the caravan. A skinny middle-aged man wearing a threadbare robe jumped out of the undergrowth in front of them. Two more men in equally shabby clothing leaped onto the trail behind Long and NgGung's cart. All three men carried makeshift *kwandos*—long wooden shafts tipped with a large wide blade on one end and a heavy metal spike on the other.

These men could not have chosen a more inappropriate weapon to wield in the narrow confines of this forest trail. A *kwando* was designed for use in an open battlefield. They would never be able to swing their weapons properly without hitting the close-packed tree trunks and endless overhanging branches.

It was apparent that these men had planned to rob them, but they were obviously amateurs. They had chosen their weapons for shock value instead of practicality. And judging from the imbalanced manner in which the lead man was holding his weapon, it was equally clear that he would not know how to use it even if he did have the room.

NgGung seemed to have noticed these things, too. He smiled and took a step forward.

"Stop!" the lead man commanded in a surprisingly strong voice. "Move away from your cart and there won't be any trouble. We do not want to hurt you."

NgGung patted the horse's nape and handed its reins over to Long. "We do not want any trouble, either, my good man," NgGung said, taking another step forward. "Why don't you find someone else to pester?"

"Don't take another step," the lead man warned. He pointed the *kwando*'s blade at NgGung's head and shook it powerfully. It was an impressive display for such a skinny man.

NgGung's smile widened. He continued toward the man, and the man seemed unsure what he should do.

NgGung stopped within reach of the man's weapon and said, "I applaud your determination, but someone is about to get hurt with that thing and it isn't going to be me." He pointed to his smashed nose and ran a finger along his battered forehead, highlighting a lifetime of combat wounds. "Do us all a favor and lower your weapon. Walk back into the forest, and pretend you never saw us. Better yet, join us. We could use men as brave as you. I could even show you how to hold that properly."

The man hesitated, and Long heard a faint scuffle behind them. He turned to see Hung and Sanfu pin the other two men to the ground with their own *kwandos*.

Long looked back at the lead man and saw that his hands were beginning to shake.

"You appear to be a reasonable individual," Ng-Gung said. "You gave us fair warning before attacking. This tells me that you are in the wrong line of business. A real thief needs to be ruthless—attack first and talk second. What is it you normally do for a living?"

The man lowered his head. "I am a baker."

"Why, that is an admirable trade!" NgGung said enthusiastically. "Much better than a thief. Do you know how to make stuffed pork buns?"

The baker lifted his head. "I make the best buns in the region. Why?"

"Excellent!" NgGung replied. "We have several hundred people in our camp, but not one of them can make a decent pork bun. You'll be a hero!"

The baker's eyes widened. "Several hundred people in your camp? Why, you must be members of the Resistance! It is an honor to meet you." He bowed. "If I may ask, what are you doing here? Rumor has it that your camp is to the south."

NgGung gestured to Long and to PawPaw, who was

now walking toward them up the trail, leading the second horse and its cart. "We are gathering recruits. Your timing could not be better. Would you like to join us?"

"Certainly," the baker said. "I believe I can speak for my friends, too."

The two men on the ground mumbled something that sounded like they agreed, and Hung and Sanfu released them.

"Do you know of any others in the area who might be interested in joining our cause?" NgGung asked.

"I believe I can bring many compatriots," the baker replied. "More than a hundred. Army enlisters sent by a new warlord called Tonglong have been overrunning nearby villages, and the only way we can avoid being forced into the army is to hide in the forest. This Tonglong's mandatory recruiting is destroying our families and our livelihoods, and his soldiers are eating up all of our winter stores. He must be dealt with."

NgGung slapped the baker on the shoulder. "Very good. Round up every man and woman you can, and gather at this spot in exactly fifteen days. Bring as much food, weapons, and other supplies as you can carry. Horses would be particularly helpful. I understand that Tonglong has been hoarding them even more than he has been hoarding recruits."

"He has," the baker said. "I will spread the word and meet you back here in fifteen days."

NgGung bowed. "It was very nice meeting you, my friend. I look forward to sampling your wares and to meeting our new recruits." He motioned to Hung. "Shall we be on our way?"

Hung grunted, and they continued up the trail.

The next several days were relatively uneventful for Long. He spent his daylight hours chatting with Ng-Gung as they walked, and his nights learning as much as he could about horses from Sanfu. Sanfu was responsible for choosing their campsites and making sure the horses had plenty to drink and graze on. While Sanfu modestly said that he was not a horse expert, he was able to give Long a good idea of how to care for and handle one.

Long would help Sanfu unhook the horses from their carts every evening, removing their collars and harnesses. He would then lash each horse's halter to the base of a stout tree, allowing enough distance between the animals for them to be able to eat and rest without harassing one another, or becoming entangled. He would also check their hooves, dislodging small stones and the like.

Before dawn, while the others were still asleep, Long would ride one of the horses bareback for a time before hooking it back to the cart. The horses were old and gentle, and he found them to be forgiving of any mistake he made. He quickly learned to steer by holding the reins and lightly moving the leather straps either right or left across their necks. The horses were far more sensitive than he had imagined, and he was soon able to turn them with little more than a flick of his wrist.

Riding atop a horse without a saddle was not the most comfortable thing in the world, but it would be better than walking a great distance, especially since his leg and arm were still on the mend. He was eager to try galloping, but there was never enough open ground to attempt it. Besides, as Sanfu had pointed out, these were stubby old Mongolian workhorses. If their cumbersome gait was uncomfortable at a walking speed, at a full gallop it would rattle his skeleton and bruise his bottom worse than anything he had ever encountered in the fight clubs.

After five days on the trail, Long was growing confident in his basic riding skills, and he could not have been more pleased, especially after they passed through a particularly dense stand of bamboo and he saw a collection of tents in a clearing ahead.

It was the bandit camp.

CHAPTER 10

ShaoShu sat atop his secondhand pony, staring through rays of fading afternoon light at the fast-moving caravan of riders ahead of him. All he had seen for the past several weeks were horses' butts, and he was sick of it. He hoped the group pitching tents ahead meant a long-term change of scenery.

As part of Tonglong's official caravan, ShaoShu and ninety-nine of Tonglong's elite soldiers were racing ahead of the main troops to the former bandit stronghold so that Tonglong could make plans with Commander Woo, the man Tonglong had left in charge. They were in such a hurry, Tonglong forbade them to set up formal camps at night. They slept beneath the stars, or in the homes of villagers they came across.

ShaoShu felt terrible about the treatment of those poor villagers. The soldiers would throw people out of their own homes and eat everything in sight, then steal whatever they chose when they left the following morning. If the villagers complained, the soldiers would burn their homes to the ground.

ShaoShu wanted it to be over soon, but he knew that it would not. Tonglong was only getting started. His network of recruiters had grown amazingly quickly because of the bounties he offered, and men and boys were being dragged into his army at a frightening pace. The recruiters' reach grew longer and faster than even Tonglong's elite caravan could travel.

As ShaoShu continued down the trail, his thoughts were interrupted by the sight of soldiers pitching tents in a large clearing. One side of the clearing was a thick line of trees. The other side was a tall stone wall that had been damaged in a few places, and beyond the wall was a series of ruined buildings. The buildings had been made of stone and were covered with burn marks. The tile roofs had gaping holes where flames had licked their way through, and all of the doors and windows had been burned away. He wondered why this location had been selected.

"Cangzhen Temple?" a nearby soldier said. "Really? No wonder Warlord Tonglong chose this spot to set up our first real camp. It represents one of his first victories, and I understand that Cangzhen is quite close to the stronghold. Maybe we will finally get a break from this insane pace."

Cangzhen Temple! ShaoShu thought. So this was

where Hok and the others had lived! He gave his pony a slap on its rump and steered it toward a crumbled section of the wall. He wanted to take a look around before someone put him to work.

ShaoShu made it through the gap without attracting any attention and jumped off his pony. What a horrible attack this must have been. Besides the burn marks, there were huge dark stains along the sides of many of the buildings that could only have been blood. He could not imagine two thousand soldiers armed with cannons and muskets attacking one hundred monks who had little more than sticks and swords.

Soldiers began to call out for ShaoShu, but he was eager to see more. He tied his pony to a piece of rubble and headed deeper into the destruction.

When he had heard about his friends growing up at Cangzhen Temple, ShaoShu had imagined one building. However, it was actually a collection of many buildings, with the high wall surrounding everything. He kept close to the wall, scurrying in its shadow, and soon reached one of the compound's back corners. Here he found a small building with something shiny on the roof. Of course, he could not resist finding out what it was. He looked around and saw a thin clay drainpipe running straight up one corner of the building. It stopped at an ornate stone dragon overhanging the roofline.

ShaoShu shinnied up the pipe, climbed over the dragon, and stopped dead in his tracks. There was another dragon on the roof, hidden behind the stone one—only this second dragon was real! It bared its pointed teeth at him, stuck out its forked tongue, and growled, "Get out!"

ShaoShu let out a small shriek and leaped back, tripping over the stone dragon. He was beginning to tumble off the roof when the real dragon stabbed its sharp claws into his collar and jerked him to safety.

The dragon clamped another claw over ShaoShu's mouth and hissed in his ear, "Hush, ShaoShu! It's me, Ying."

ShaoShu felt the pressure released from his mouth and collar, and he stared. It was indeed Ying.

"I apologize," Ying said. "I did not recognize you at first."

ShaoShu shrugged. He was not sure if he should be frightened or ecstatic. "What are you doing here?" he asked.

"I might ask you the same thing. However, I think I can guess what is happening. Tonglong is stopping here on the way to the Forbidden City."

"Actually, he is stopping here on his way to the bandits' former stronghold. We are going to wait there with a man named Commander Woo until the troops arrive from the south and east."

"Nice work," Ying said. "What else do you know?"

"Lots of things," ShaoShu replied. "For one, Tonglong is a very bad man. Sometimes, when he wants information from someone and they won't give it to him, he tortures them by—"

"I can imagine," Ying interrupted. "Look, we do not have much time to talk. Can you give me any specific troop information? How many men does Tonglong have?"

"Ninety-nine. He calls them his 'elite force.' They are nasty, and they love to use pistols. They wear red uniforms like the one I am wearing, and like the Southern army wears."

"How many men is he expecting to arrive later?"

"No one knows for sure. He has tens of thousands already, and he gets more every day. It is unbelievable."

Ying spat. "This is far more serious than I thought. The Forbidden City has its own sizable force, but I believe it is only a few thousand men. Tonglong might be able to overrun it with sheer numbers. I need to get to him before he reaches the Forbidden City. You said that he is going to see Commander Woo now?"

"I believe so," ShaoShu said.

"Do you know anything about their short-term plans?"

"One man Tonglong tortured told him that the bandits are training a rebel army. Tonglong wants to hunt them down and exterminate them before he gets to the Forbidden City."

"Thank you, ShaoShu. This helps a lot. You are

very brave for staying with Tonglong all this time. Do you have any news about the Emperor?"

"Tonglong has captured him and is keeping him alive at least until we get to the Forbidden City. Everyone knows that the Emperor is traveling with Tonglong, but they think the Emperor is traveling in style with the main army. We are actually transporting him secretly, against his will, in a crate built to carry pigs. It stinks so bad no one goes near it. He is all alone inside. I sneak him extra food and water every once in a while, even though I have been punished once for doing it."

"That is very kind of you," Ying said. "What about Hok and the others?"

"Seh is supposed to be with the bandits, and Hok, Malao, and Fu were going to try to find him. I bet Long went with them, plus a man called Xie, who was the Emperor's personal bodyguard. Tonglong killed Xie's father—the Western Warlord. Tonglong even killed his own mother, AnGangseh. He is heartless."

Ying scowled. "This is unbelievable. I have been alone in the mountains and knew almost none of this. I need to find the bandits and give them an update as soon as possible. Do you know where they might be?"

"No. Tonglong plans to ask Commander Woo the same question when we get to the stronghold. What were you doing in the mountains?"

"Practicing."

"Practicing what?"

Ying reached behind him and lifted a rusty straight sword from the rooftop. The blade was covered with scaly clumps of orange and red, but the handle was shiny and gold and covered with entwined dragons. While ShaoShu hated weapons, he considered this one beautiful. It must have been what had caught his eye while he was on the ground.

"Wow," ShaoShu said. "Is that yours?"

"I suppose it is now," Ying replied in a sad tone. "It belonged to the Grandmaster of this temple, my grandfather. I threw it up here after I killed him, so that it could die, too. I have decided to try to breathe life back into it. Perhaps it will help me right some of my wrongs."

ShaoShu did not know what to say. He looked away to avoid eye contact with Ying, and noticed a soldier headed in their direction. Fortunately, the man seemed to be looking inside the buildings, not up on the rooftops. He shouted into the doorway of a nearby structure, "ShaoShu! Where are you, you little rodent? I am not in the mood for hide-and-seek. Get out here and give us a hand!"

"Uh-oh," ShaoShu said. "I had better get going."

Ying nodded. "It was good seeing you."

"You too." ShaoShu turned to go, then stopped and reached deep into the folds of his robe. He pulled out the two dragon scrolls he had stolen from Tonglong, and held them out for Ying. "I almost forgot these. Maybe you can use them. One even has sketches of a guy holding a sword like your grandfather's in one hand, and a chain whip like yours in the other hand."

Ying's eyes widened and he took the scrolls from ShaoShu, unrolling them quickly. When Ying saw the sketches of the figure with a sword and a chain whip, ShaoShu swore that he was going to kiss him. Fortunately, Ying only patted him on the head.

"You amaze me," Ying whispered with a wide grin, but then he frowned.

"What?" ShaoShu asked.

"I just realized that Tonglong will have read this scroll. He will be familiar with the techniques shown in it. No matter. Knowing what the enemy knows is half the battle. Get out of here, my little friend. You have given me more than I deserve."

ShaoShu beamed. He gave Ying a quick wave and scurried back down the drainpipe to rejoin Tonglong's men.

CHAPTER
12

Seh felt the newcomer's stare from across the bandit camp. His flesh began to tingle, and the hair on the back of his neck stood on end. While his vision continued to improve, he did not need his eyes to know who had just arrived. Only a dragon could project that much energy.

Seh bowed to the thirty spear-wielding students around him, and he dismissed them with a wave of his hand. The students returned the bow and hurried off.

Seh focused his gaze in the direction of the camp's only trailhead. It was his brother Long, accompanied by NgGung, Hung, and PawPaw. They had two horse-drawn carts with them. Long handed the reins of one of the horses to NgGung, and he waved to Seh. Seh waved back, a smile on his face.

"You can see us?" PawPaw called out to Seh in an astonished tone.

"Yes," Seh replied. "Your dragon bone treatment is working miracles. Thank you."

"Excellent!" PawPaw said. "How much do you have left?"

"Between what you have given me and the large amount Hok brought, I believe I have enough to last three hundred and fifty years!"

PawPaw laughed. "That is good news. I suppose I will not have to worry about finding more for you, then. It is scarce enough as it is. Is your father here?"

"Yes. He is in his tent."

"Very good. NgGung, Hung, and I need to speak with him immediately. I suppose you would like to visit with your older brother?"

"Nothing would please me more."

Hung, NgGung, and PawPaw headed for a large tent in the center of camp, and Long came over to Seh. Long was grinning, but he had a strange expression on his face. He stared at Seh.

"It is good to see you again, Brother Seh," Long said finally.

"Likewise," Seh replied.

Long stared again.

"Is there something bothering you?" Seh asked. "My appearance, perhaps?"

"It confuses me," Long said. "Your presence feels the same, but you look very different with hair. You resemble Tonglong from a distance, but now that I see you up close, you look a surprising amount like your mother. Not to worry, I will grow used to it."

Seh frowned. "I do not wish to look like either one. You are not the first person to say these things. I am considering shaving my head like we used to at Cangzhen Temple."

"Maybe you should, only then you may look like your father."

"He *is* bald, but I will never look like him. No one does. Sometimes I wish I were more like Fu, who looks a lot like his father. And you should see Hok with her mother, Bing, as well as Hok's little sister, GongJee. They all look alike, and they are all very nice individuals."

"Are they here?" Long asked.

"Only GongJee is. Fu, Malao, Hok, Bing, and a few others have gone out on a reconnaissance mission to the bandits' former stronghold. There has been a lot of activity reported in that area recently."

"Tonglong's troops?"

"We think so. Or at least a small portion of his troops. What it means for us is that we may have to move our camp—again. I have only been here a few months, and we have already moved three times. This camp may not look like much, but it is an unbelievable amount of work packing up and moving."

Long nodded, and Seh watched him gaze from tent to tattered tent.

"There are a few hundred of us here," Seh said. "But large groups of men join us every week. We spend nearly all of our time preparing for war—carving spear shafts, sharpening weapons, and forging pistol balls, even though we have few firearms."

"It sounds hectic," Long said.

"It is. It's a tense, nervous environment, with everyone constantly on edge, waiting for the inevitable battle to begin. Sometimes I grow exhausted just watching everyone storm about, negative energy surging from their bodies like summer heat lightning."

Long frowned. "Grandmaster once told me that it was like this around the time we were born."

"My father told me the same thing. I now understand why he chose to give me up to Grandmaster, and why Hok's parents eventually did the same thing. This is no place for children."

Seh heard NgGung call out for them to come to Mong's tent, and Long said, "That was fast."

"My father hates to waste time," Seh replied.

Seh and Long walked over to the largest tent in the camp and found the bandit leader sitting cross-legged in the center of a threadbare carpet that filled the space from wall to wall. NgGung, Sanfu, Hung, and PawPaw sat on either side of him, and Mong motioned for Seh and Long to sit in front of the group. Seh glanced out of the corner of his eye and caught Long looking his father over.

Seh could not blame him for staring. His father was gigantic. Mong's shoulders rippled beneath his robes, reminding most people of a python swallowing its prey. He was also pale and strangely hairless. Not only was he bald, with no eyebrows to speak of, but there was not a single hair on the backs of his hands or even his forearms.

While Mong's appearance was imposing, he gave off a positive energy that immediately put a person at ease. Seh felt Long begin to relax, and he watched as Long bowed respectfully.

"Welcome, young dragon," Mong said in his deep, powerful voice. "Do you remember me?"

"Yes, sir," Long replied. "I recall seeing you at Cangzhen Temple. Grandmaster never said much about you, but NgGung told me a great deal on our trek here."

Mong nodded. "Are you well? I understand that you have been injured. Tales of your fight at the Shanghai Fight Club have made you a hero. Defeating a man armed with pistols and a knife while you were weaponless is extremely impressive. Congratulations."

"Thank you," Long said, sounding somewhat embarrassed. "I have nearly recovered from my wounds, thanks to PawPaw and my sister, Hok."

"Very glad to hear it," Mong said. "Let us get down to business. I have had a discussion with your companions here, and of course your temple siblings told me a great deal upon their arrival weeks ago. You have a task ahead of you, and the road you must follow is an obvious one. We need to get you to Xie as soon as possible. Are you still willing to go?"

"Yes, sir."

"Excellent. Here is how things will unfold. NgGung

will outfit you with any necessary supplies, and you will travel with him on foot to the city of Kaifeng. He knows how to find the man, Cang, whom you were told to seek. Cang has very good relations with the local politicians and has not had to give up his horses to Tonglong's troops. Cang will give you the best horse you can imagine for the remainder of your travels. Your journey to Tunhuang will be difficult, but I have faith in your skills. You are young, resilient, and strong, and you have already proved your resourcefulness in hand-to-hand combat, if things should come to that."

Long nodded.

"Once you locate Xie," Mong said, "tell him that he must commence to the Forbidden City immediately with his armies to reinforce the troops there. Xie was the Emperor's personal bodyguard, so the palace staff should listen when he speaks. We will have only one chance to stop Tonglong. I shall meet Xie at the main gates of the Forbidden City one week before New Year's Eve to discuss whatever battle plan he sees fit. My forces will be ready at that time, and I hope to have between three thousand and five thousand trained men and women by then."

"New Year's, sir?" Long said. "That is months away."

"From what I understand, Tonglong's main body of troops is pushing ahead at a steady pace, and its current rate of movement will put him at the Forbidden City just in time for the New Year celebrations. I believe that a New Year takeover is Tonglong's goal. It would be highly symbolic and in keeping with Tonglong's flair for the dramatic. Is all of this clear to you?"

"It is, sir. What should I do after I give Xie this information?"

"Stay with him. We will likely move again soon, and I, for one, will be difficult to find. Any more questions?"

"No, sir."

"Go with NgGung, then. You will leave immediately."

Long's eyebrows rose. "Immediately, sir?"

"Is that a problem?"

"I was hoping to see my temple siblings. Seh informed me that they are on a reconnaissance mission to your former stronghold. Do you know when they might return?"

"Not for several days," Mong replied. "You will have to wait until we all reach the Forbidden City to see them again."

Long sighed. "I understand. Please give them my regards."

"Of course."

Long stood and bowed to the group. Seh and Ng-Gung stood, too.

"Follow me, boys," NgGung said, and they followed him out. NgGung hurried across the camp. Seh found that he and Long had to jog to keep pace with him. For a man with such stubby legs, NgGung sure moved fast.

When they reached the last row of tents, NgGung headed for a moldy old one off to one side that was small, dirty, and dank. No matter where they set up camp, NgGung was always made to pitch his tent at the point furthest downwind from the prevailing winds. Seh saw Long wrinkle his nose.

Seh whispered to Long, "It smells worse than Malao's feet in there. Enter at your own risk."

"Home sweet home!" NgGung said with a grin. "Come on in."

"No, thank you," Long replied. "I think I will wait out here."

"Suit yourself," NgGung said. "I'll be right back."

NgGung headed inside and soon emerged with an armload of clothes. He dropped them in the dirt and began to sort them out, using his nose as the main criterion for grouping the items. When he had finished his sniffing and sorting, he pointed to the smallest pile. "Those are for you. I wouldn't recommend the others."

"I will take your word for it," Long said. "Thank you."

"Don't mention it. You can give them a quick wash in the horse trough if you'd like, but personally I think they're fine. Too fine, in fact. I don't think I've ever worn them. They were gifts, but I hate silk. Too slippery."

Seh watched Long lean over the smallest pile and take a quick sniff. He picked up the clothes and smiled. "These are very nice," Long said. "I am no clothing expert, but they look expensive. They smell just fine, too."

Long disappeared behind a tree, reappearing as a new person. The brown silk pants and matching robe fit him surprisingly well, as did a fur-lined black silk jacket.

"Very nice," NgGung said. "Now, just a few more items—" He headed into his tent once again, coming out with a pair of leather boots, heavy leather gloves, a fur-lined leather hat, and a short knife in a small sheath.

Long appeared speechless. He took the items and tried them on, and to Seh everything appeared to fit well. Long seemed pleased, but held the knife out to NgGung. "I am sorry, but this is one thing I cannot take."

"Sure you can," NgGung said. "It is nothing, really. Those boots cost more than that knife. I am almost ashamed to give it to you. However, I noticed that you don't carry one. You need to change that."

"You do not understand," Long said. "I dislike weapons."

"It's not a weapon," NgGung said. "It's a survival tool. You should *never* travel alone without one. Cang won't even let you get up on one of his horses without something sharp handy. What if you or your horse gets tangled up in something? Horses have all sorts of ropes hanging off them. Knives are for cutting more than just people, you know."

Long blushed. "You are right. I am sorry."

"Don't be sorry. Just slip it behind your sash and forget about it. You won't even know it's there. I need to grab a few things from our storage tent, and we'll be on our way."

NgGung hurried off, and Long slipped the knife

between his robe sash and the small of his back. He turned to Seh.

"I guess this is it, Brother," Long said.

"So it is," Seh replied. "It is the beginning of something big. I can feel it."

Long nodded. "I feel it, too. Please give Fu, Malao, and Hok my best wishes."

"Give them your wishes yourself. We shall see you at the Forbidden City."

"Do you think so?"

"I know so."

Long and NgGung made excellent time traveling over the next four days on their way to Kaifeng. They slept little and ate even less, but Long still enjoyed himself. NgGung was an interesting companion, and he knew the region like the back of his hand. He knew exactly how far they were to travel each day, and where the best rock shelters and tree hollows were for spending each night. They made a few stops for water, but those were rare, as they each carried over their shoulders a pair of large water skins that Long was to use on his trek across the desert to Tunhuang.

In addition to the water skins, NgGung had provided Long with a saddlebag packed with dried meats and fruits for his journey, as well as a map. NgGung said that it was a thousand *li* from Kaifeng to Tunhuang, and that it would take a person at least thirty days to make the trip on foot. With a normal horse, it could be done in ten days, but with one of Cang's "Heavenly Horses," it could be done in five or six. Cang's horses were renowned for their speed as well as their stamina. Now that he'd had some experience on horseback, Long could not wait to ride one.

They arrived at the southern edge of Kaifeng well after nightfall on the fourth day, which suited NgGung just fine. He knew this city as intimately as he knew the countryside, and they slipped unseen through back alleyways and little-traveled side streets until they'd passed clear through the southern half of the city to its midpoint at the Yellow River's icy waters. There they turned west, following the river upstream for hours in the cold before reaching the city's outskirts as the sun finally began to rise and bring them some welcome warmth.

In the growing daylight, Long saw a waist-high fence ahead that stretched from the riverbank inland as far as he could see. He pointed a gloved finger at the seemingly endless line. "What could possibly need that much room to run?"

"You will find out soon enough," NgGung said. "That is Cang's pasture."

"Impressive," Long replied. "Where are his stables?"

"Several *li* upriver. This is the easternmost edge of his land."

"How long will it take us to get there?"

"Get there? I don't know. Few people have seen his stables. He has always come to me. He rides his fences every morning, checking for sections damaged by weather or rustlers in the night. It is too early for him to have come this far yet, so if we just wait here, he will see us soon enough. In the meantime, relax. This may be the last opportunity you'll have to get some sleep for quite a while."

NgGung set his water skins and travel bag down, and took a seat on top of the fence. He pointed to the thick grass inside the fence line.

Long got the point. He set his items next to Ng-Gung's, climbed over the fence, and lay down atop the soft grass in the warm sun. He fell asleep almost instantly. Three hours passed before he was woken by the sound of hooves pounding against the earth.

Long sat up and saw a man atop a beautiful black horse, tearing along the fence line toward them at an amazing rate. The horse was much taller and thinner than the bandits' workhorses and had a lot less hair. It was sleek and beautifully proportioned, and even from a distance Long could see a wild gleam in its eye.

"Here comes Cang," NgGung said.

Long continued to stare at the horse, and before he knew it, it was nearly upon him. Moreover, it did not look like it was going to slow down. Its hooves would grind him to a pulp if he did not move.

Long threw himself over the fence. At the same

instant, Cang called out, "Whoa!" and Long saw him pull back on the reins, bringing the animal to a skidding halt a handbreadth from where Long had just been lying.

Cang looked over at NgGung and winked, then NgGung burst into laughter, slapping his thigh. "No matter how many times I see you do that, it never gets old! Hilarious!"

Long frowned. He did not find it the least bit funny. Even so, he looked up at Cang and got the feeling that he was a decent man, regardless of his strange sense of humor. Cang nodded a greeting, and Long bowed respectfully.

Long straightened and glanced at Cang's horse. He was surprised to see that even though it had just been running extremely hard, it did not look the least bit winded. In fact, it had not even broken a sweat.

As for Cang, he was different from what Long had been expecting. The horseman was old and thin, with wild long white hair that streamed behind him in thin wisps. Nearly all of his teeth were missing, and his face was as brown and rugged as an old leather boot. However, his eyes were traced with laugh lines, which softened his appearance greatly. Even though he had just scared the life out of Long, Long could not be angry with the man.

"Greetings," Cang said to Long. "I have been expecting you. Or at least I think you are the one I am expecting. Xie told me that someone meeting your description would be coming my way. Do you have any means of identifying yourself?"

Long removed his heavy leather gloves and held up his left thumb. The ring Xie had given him glistened in the late-morning sun.

"There it is," Cang said. "The mark of my lord. You must be the chosen one." He winked.

"Your lord?" Long asked.

"My warlord, if you prefer. My leader. I may live in Kaifeng with its bountiful grass and endless supply of water, but I consider myself a loyal subject of Xie's desert family. Since his father has passed away, I now serve Xie."

"What about the Emperor?"

"Xie's family roots run much deeper than those of the ever-changing Forbidden City. In the city of Tun-huang, the Western Warlord is much more revered than the Emperor."

Long had had no idea Xie was so powerful. He eyed Cang's magnificent horse, and Cang smiled. "Have you ever ridden a horse, young man?"

"A little, sir."

"How many different horses?"

"Two."

"What kind were they?"

"Workhorses."

"What kind of workhorses?"

Long thought for a moment. "Old ones."

Cang chuckled. "I mean, what breed were they?"

"I am sorry, I do not know."

"That is what I guessed you might say. Do you have any idea what you are in for?"

Long's shoulders slumped. "Probably not."

Cang's eyebrows furrowed and he locked eyes with Long. "How old are you?"

"Thirteen."

"By the looks of you, I would have guessed older—perhaps sixteen. I am not sure you are ready for a journey like this. However, I will give you a chance. Prove to me that you can ride, and I will help you."

Long breathed a sigh of relief. "Thank you, sir."

"Thank me later. First, I need to make sure you won't kill yourself." Cang began to swing himself out of the saddle.

Long's eyes widened. "You want me to ride *that* horse? Right now?"

"Yes," Cang said. He hopped off the horse like a man half his age and handed the reins to Long. "Let us see what you can do."

Long looked at the horse with its saddle and stirrups. "I have only ridden bareback, sir."

"Did you use reins?"

Long nodded.

"What about kung fu?"

"Excuse me, sir?"

"Have you ever practiced kung fu?"

Long stared at Cang, dumbfounded. "You could say that I know a little about the topic."

NgGung laughed out loud. "That's pretty funny, Long."

Long ignored him.

"All right," Cang said. "I take it you know how to do a Horse Stance?"

"Yes."

"Here is what you are going to do, then. Get up on the horse and put your feet in the stirrups on either side of the animal. Then lower yourself into a Horse Stance—or Horseback Riding Stance, as some kung fu instructors call it—and use your legs as springs to help absorb the shock of the horse in motion. It will be hard on your thighs, and even your stomach and back muscles, but the longer your tail is up off the saddle, the less bruising and saddle sores you are going to get. Understand?"

"Yes, sir."

"Good. Now, your legs cannot hold you up like that all day long, so you are going to have to get a feel for when you can sit and when you should not. It will take time, but you will figure it out."

"I understand."

"Do you? Get up there and show me."

Long turned to face the horse's left side, taking the reins in his left hand. He placed his left foot in the stirrup, sprang into the air off his right leg, and raised his right leg high, swinging it forward in order to throw it over the horse's back. Unfortunately, the horse was no longer there. It was leaping sideways away from him.

Long felt himself falling backward, and there was nothing he could do. He dropped his chin to his chest to protect the back of his head and hit the ground high on his upper back, his left foot still stuck in the stirrup and the reins still in his hand. Fortunately, the horse did not run off. It just stood there, looking back at him.

Cang rushed over and took the reins from Long. NgGung hopped off the fence, pulling Long's boot free of the stirrup. Long sat up and felt his wounded right thigh begin to throb. "What just happened?" he asked.

"Rule number one," Cang said. "Pay close attention to the reins. When you hopped into the air, you let your left hand drop. The reins are attached to something called a bit, which is a piece of metal between the horse's teeth. Pulling down like that hurts."

"Sorry," Long said. He stood and brushed himself off. "Lesson learned."

"Hmpf," Cang muttered, handing the reins back to Long.

Long tried mounting the horse again, this time paying close attention to the reins. He made it up and into the saddle in one smooth motion. He glanced over at NgGung, who had climbed back onto the fence, and NgGung nodded his approval.

Long turned to see Cang's reaction and felt his weight shift to one side. His new silk pants caused him to slip wildly in the smooth leather saddle, and he squeezed his thighs against the horse's sides in an effort to regain his balance.

The horse took off.

"Hey!" Long yelled as they trotted inland along the fence line. Slipping worse now because of the bouncing gait, Long fought the urge to pull on the reins for support. He did not know if this would hurt the horse or not, but he took a chance and grabbed a handful of mane, heaving himself to a balanced sitting position.

The horse seemed fine with it, and Long gave a sigh of relief.

Unfortunately, they were now moving along at a fairly quick pace, and he was still slipping every which way, even with his feet in the stirrups. Maintaining a Horse Stance, as Cang had said, seemed to help, but keeping both of his feet parallel to the ground was proving to be far more difficult than he had imagined, because the horse rocked from side to side with every step.

Long repositioned his body repeatedly in an effort to find which posture worked best, but had little success. Hunching forward and bringing his heels up did not help. Leaning backward and pushing his legs forward was even worse. But eventually, he figured out that it was best if he kept his body in a straight line, perpendicular to the ground, just like in a proper kung fu stance. He kept his legs long, dropped his heels, and aligned his ears, shoulders, and hips with his heels. It worked like a charm.

Once he was confident going forward, Long decided to work on turning the horse. Cang and NgGung were already out of sight, and he needed to turn the horse 180 degrees to the right, because the fence was still close on his left. He slid the reins across the horse's neck to his right, and the horse began to turn in a large arc.

Things were going well until there came a point

when the horse's changing angle caused his silk pants to slip again. He pressed his right leg against the horse's right side in order to maintain his balance, and the horse suddenly turned hard in that direction, nearly throwing Long from the saddle. He instinctively squeezed both legs hard to keep himself atop the horse, and the horse bolted again, this time breaking into a full gallop.

Long threw himself forward and wrapped his arms around the horse's neck, hanging on for dear life. The horse whinnied loudly and snorted, running like mad along the fence line toward the river. In less time than Long thought possible, he saw Cang and NgGung straight ahead. Both men were gesturing frantically, motioning for him to pull back on the reins.

Long reluctantly released his grip on the horse's neck and gripped the reins as best he could. He jerked them backward, perhaps a bit too hard, and the horse stopped dead in its tracks, dropping its head.

Between Long's forward momentum and his slippery pants, he shot forward over the horse's lowered head like a New Year's firework. He tucked into a roll that would have made an acrobat proud, bounced across the soft pasture grass three times, then popped onto his feet. He rubbed the old wounds on his sore right leg and left shoulder, and looked at Cang.

Cang began to laugh so hard tears ran down his leathery face. "I have been watching people ride for more years than I can count, and that had to be the worst dismount I have ever seen. Congratulations."

Long frowned and looked at NgGung. NgGung was laughing almost as hard as Cang.

Long kicked the dirt and walked over to the horse. It stared back at him as though nothing had happened.

"What is wrong with this crazy animal?" Long asked.

"Why do you think something is wrong?" Cang said, wiping away tears. "He is one of the best horses I have ever worked with. You do not even need to hold the reins with this one. You can control his speed and steer simply by using your legs. It is a trick the Mongolians use out on the plains so that they can ride their horses and shoot their bows at the same time."

Long thought for a moment and realized what had happened. "So if I press one leg into the horse's side, it will turn in that direction, and if I squeeze both legs at the same time, it will go faster?"

Cang's eyes sparkled. "That is correct. You are a fast learner. The way you handled those falls was impressive, too. I think you will be fine, even with those silly pants."

Long looked down at his legs. The fine silk was now as dirty as anything NgGung had pulled out of his tent, and the clothes no longer smelled much better than NgGung's, either. He was beginning to reek of horse.

Cang waved something in his hands, and Long saw that he was holding the map NgGung had given him.

"NgGung pulled this from your saddlebag while

you were out proving yourself," Cang said. "There are many routes to Tunhuang, but I believe this is indeed the best one for you to take, as it is the shortest. However, it is also the most desolate. There are no cities or villages along the way, only a small outpost on the edge of the great Gobi Desert. If I give you one of my horses, you must agree to stop there. The outpost is little more than an inn with a small blacksmith shop, and the owner is my friend. His name is DingXiang, and he has a great knowledge of horses' hooves. Tell him that I sent you, and ask him to inspect the horse. I never shoe my horses, but where you are going the terrain is much different. Show him your map, and he will determine what course of action should be taken, if any. Ask him to sell you a pair of riding pants, too. You do have money, don't you?"

"I have a little," Long replied.

"A little will be all you need. DingXiang will not charge you for attending to GuangZe."

"*GuangZe?*" Long asked. "Sheen? Luster? What does that mean?"

"That is the name of the horse you just rode. I had a different one picked out for you, but I think you should take him. He is afraid of loud noises, but otherwise is a very reliable mount. Best of all, I believe he likes you. I can walk back to my stables."

"Likes me?" Long asked, looking over at the horse. It still had that intense gleam in its eye. "How do you know?"

"He has not tried to bite you."

"Horses *bite*?"

Cang groaned. "You really do not know what you are getting yourself into, do you? Get out of here before I change my mind."

CHAPTER 14

Long rode faster than the wind, crossing *li* upon *li* of open grassland. At first, he loved every moment of it. It felt as though he were flying, the ride igniting feelings he had never known were locked away inside him. It must have been his inner dragon, soaring for the first time.

The feeling didn't last long. The farther he rode, the more uncomfortable he became. The terrain quickly grew arid, and cold, dry breezes made his skin crack. He began to see pockets of barren earth dusted with sand, the sand somehow managing to find its way deep into his eyes, ears, nose, and hair, even though he wore a hat pulled down over his head and most of his face. Fortunately, GuangZe seemed immune to these discomforts.

On his third day out, he reached the outpost and

the edge of the Gobi Desert, where there was nothing to the west but sand as far as he could see. It was a strange place, this desert in the north. While he had previously associated deserts with tales Grandmaster had shared of hot places, here on the fringes it was beginning to snow.

The outpost itself was little more than two weather-beaten buildings, one fairly large and one small. Thick smoke poured out of a chimney attached to the small one, and Long heard the sound of metal being hammered within. That was obviously Ding-Xiang's blacksmith shop.

Attached to one side of the larger building was a small stable containing three squat Mongolian horses. Long headed for the stable in the approaching dusk, and his *dan tien* began to warm. There were people inside.

As Long neared, two short men stepped out of the stable's shadowed interior. They were covered from head to toe in tattered black silk, their faces hidden by an extension of the black turbans on their heads. The only thing showing was their narrow eyes. Each man held a long, curved sword unlike any Long had ever seen. The swords were sheathed, but held in an aggressive manner.

Long did not want any trouble. However, if there was to be some, the last place he wanted to be was atop a horse. He dismounted quickly and tied GuangZe to a post as the men approached. One of them said in heavily accented Mandarin Chinese, "That is a fine animal."

"Thank you," Long replied, unable to determine what country the man came from. "Do you know where I can find DingXiang the blacksmith?"

"He is not here."

Long pointed toward the small building. "Who is in there, then?"

"His apprentice, but he is very busy right now. Perhaps we can help you?"

"I appreciate your offer, but I prefer to wait for DingXiang."

"He is not expected back for many hours. What is it you need from him?"

Long did not reply.

The man turned away from Long and looked at GuangZe. "That sure is a fine animal," he said again. "Would you consider selling him?"

"No."

"We would be willing to give you a handsome sum for him, along with one of our horses so that you would still have transportation. Where are you headed? Tunhuang?"

Long didn't answer.

"Of course you are. There is no other reason to be out here. Our horses know the way to Tunhuang blindfolded. They have spent their entire lives upon the sands. You would be much better off with one of them."

"No, thank you."

"Are you sure?"

"Positive."

The man shook his turbaned head and nodded toward his companion. "I guess we will have to take it by force, then." Both men drew their swords and advanced toward Long.

Long was not surprised. He glanced toward the stable, hoping to see a pitchfork or shovel or some other implement to help him fend off an attack, but the walls were bare.

As the men neared, Long's eyes fell upon the stable door. Tall and wide, it slid along a track hung across the top of the door. A cord ran through the track, one end tied to the door, the other tied to a small counterweight. This counterweight made the door easier to open and close.

It might also help save Long's life.

When the men were three steps from Long, he grabbed the half-filled water skins slung over Guang-Ze's rump and hurled the containers at his attackers. The men turned to protect their faces, and the water skins collided harmlessly with their backs and shoulders. By the time they straightened and poised once more for attack, however, Long had reached the door.

He leaped up and grabbed hold of the cord near the center of its length. As he came back down, the counterweight went up, stopping abruptly when it reached the first pulley.

The cord snapped in Long's hand, just as he had hoped. He released his grip and let the counterweight fall to the ground, the broken cord snaking out of the pulleys and landing in a pile on top of the counter-weight.

Long grabbed the broken end of the cord as his two attackers sprang into action. Coiling the cord in his left hand, he took the counterweight in his right and cocked his right arm back. When the first attacker was within range, Long hurled the counterweight at the man's head, letting the cord out while maintaining a tight grip on its end.

It was a direct hit. The man dropped to his knees and the cord went slack. However, the man was only dazed. His turban had absorbed more of the impact than Long would have liked.

Long switched the end of the cord to his right hand. He took several steps backward to make additional space between him and the second approaching man, and swung his right arm in a wide arc, the counterweight lifting off the ground and flying through the air like the weighted end of a chain whip or, more precisely, a rope dart.

Long had always been quite skilled with the chain whip and rope dart. Both mimicked the powerful sweeping motions of a dragon's tail. He aimed the airborne counterweight at the second attacker's head, and the man raised his sword in front of his face in an effort to protect himself.

The swinging counterweight wrapped the cord around the weapon's hilt. Long gave a vicious yank, pulling the sword from the astonished man's hands.

Long glanced at the first attacker and saw that he

had stumbled to the stable and was fumbling with a saddlebag. He produced a pistol and aimed it at Long's chest.

"I should have used this from the start," the man said. "Drop the rope and—"

Long's *dan tien* began to twitch. He heard hooves pounding behind him. He turned to see an elderly man much like Cang roar past on what appeared to be a Heavenly Horse. The rider halted in a cloud of dust in front of the stable and pulled two pistols from his sash. He pointed one at the armed man inside the stable, and the other at the unarmed man.

"Drop the pistol," the rider said to the man in the stable.

"I don't think so, DingXiang," the man in the stable replied. "I believe this is a stalemate."

"Think again," said a new voice from behind the stable. Long looked over to see a young man step around the corner carrying a pistol in one hand and a pair of glowing blacksmith tongs in the other. He dropped the tongs in the sand and positioned himself so that the man in the stable could not shoot or even see him, but he still had an easy shot at the weaponless attacker.

The weaponless attacker swallowed hard and called out to his companion inside the stable, "It's the apprentice and he's got a pistol aimed at my head. Do as he says. That horse is not worth dying for."

The man inside the stable cursed and returned his pistol to the saddlebag. He tied the bag closed and looked at DingXiang. "Satisfied?"

"I will be satisfied when the two of you leave. Take your horses and do not return."

Both did as directed. They climbed onto their horses and left, the disarmed man not even bothering to ask for his sword back.

The apprentice stepped forward from the rear of the stable. Long saw that he was about seventeen years old.

Long bowed to him and to DingXiang. "Thank you both," he said. "I feel like I should repay you somehow."

"It was nothing," DingXiang said. "Unfortunately, these events occur often out here. One must accept it as a normal part of life. I see you have a Heavenly Horse. Is it one of Cang's? GuangZe, perhaps?"

"It is GuangZe."

"A very fine horse. I suppose you are in need of some shoes for him?"

"That will be up to you, sir. I am traveling to Tunhuang."

"Of course you are. Why else would you bother to stop here? Have you selected a route yet?"

"I have a map."

"Well, let's take a look. What we put on the horse's hooves, if anything, will be dictated by the surfaces you will travel over. From here, it looks like there is nothing but sand out there forever, but once you travel west a few hours, you will begin to see rock formations. I hope your map is a good one. By good, I mean recent."

"Why?"

"There have been a number of rock slides out there

lately. Some of the passes are now blocked. My apprentice here knows the most about them. He gets updates from travelers who stop in here. Show him what you have."

Long walked over to GuangZe, impressed that the horse had remained more or less calm this entire time. He removed the map from his saddlebag and handed it to the apprentice.

"Interesting choice," the apprentice said. "This route is seldom used, but as far as I know it is still open. You should not have any problems."

"What about horseshoes?" Long asked.

DingXiang looked at the map again. "I recommend removable hoof boots instead of fixed metal horseshoes. Your route is mostly sand. Sand can wreak havoc in a freshly shod hoof if it gets beneath the shoes. Hoof boots will give your horse protection over the rocks, but you can remove them when you pass through sand."

"I have never heard of hoof boots."

"People were using them a thousand years before metal shoes," Cang said. "They are still quite common out here. They are made of leather and cloth, and secured with ties. Simple yet effective. They are custom-made for each hoof, but I can have a set for you first thing tomorrow. Enjoy a good night's rest at my inn, free of charge. And if you don't mind my saying so, you could do with a proper pair of riding pants. We appear to be roughly the same size. I will find you some."

Long bowed. "You are too kind. Thank you. I still feel like I should repay you somehow."

The apprentice grinned and nodded toward the foreigner's curved sword, lying on the ground. "If you feel that strongly about the need to repay us—or at least repay *me*—you could let me keep that sword. It does not appear to have been made in China, and I would enjoy examining its construction."

"My pleasure," Long said. He walked over and picked up the sword, unwrapping the cord and counterweight from the hilt. "Sorry about your door," he said. "Allow me to fix it."

"You will do nothing but rest while you are here," DingXiang said. "My word on that is final."

Long nodded his thanks and looked the sword over, running his finger across a large, fresh nick in the blade. He turned to the apprentice. "The iron counterweight seems to have damaged the sword in this spot."

"So much the better," the apprentice said. "A notch like that should reveal the folded layers of metal within. I am eager to examine it, but I must take this horse out for some exercise first." He took the sword from Long and gave his own bow of thanks. Then he untethered and climbed atop the remaining Mongolian horse in the stable and rode off with a big wave and an even bigger smile.

"I had better get to work," DingXiang said. "For what it is worth, Warlord Xie stopped here a few weeks ago and told me to expect you. I did not want to say anything in front of my apprentice because it is none of his business. I want you to know that I have great respect for what you are doing. Now go inside and get as much rest as you can. You are going to need it."

CHAPTER 15

Long woke the next morning feeling rested. He ate a quick breakfast, changed into a pair of heavy cloth riding pants, and followed DingXiang outside to receive instructions on how and when to use GuangZe's custom hoof boots. GuangZe was very accommodating, and within half an hour the lesson was over. Long slipped the boots into his saddlebag, waved goodbye to DingXiang, and rode into the Gobi's seemingly endless sea of half-frozen sand.

GuangZe's hooves sank deeply into the shifting sands. The poor animal had to work several times harder than normal for every step he took. Long was happy to see that the sand did not deter the horse, but it did make GuangZe wary, and he changed his gait considerably. Between the shifting sand and his new pants, Long felt like he was learning to ride all over again.

After half a day, Long was finally getting used to the new riding motions when the terrain began to change. The ground beneath GuangZe grew firm, and massive rock beds rose ahead of them out of the sand. Long stopped to put on GuangZe's hoof boots, drink some water from his water skins, and check his map.

The map included crude sketches of major rock formations to serve as reference points, and Long felt fortunate that even after the recent rock slides, he was able to figure out where he was. Up to this point, he had been attempting to ride due west, using the sun as his only compass point. Judging from the map, he had veered a fair amount to the north. This turned out to be just fine, because north was the direction of the pass he was supposed to take through the rocks.

He saw the pass less than half a *li* away and grinned. Though the deep sand was slowing them down, they were still making excellent time. By his calculation, they would reach Tunhuang in three days or less. He had more than enough food and water to get him there, and the fur-lined coat and hat NgGung had given him were doing an admirable job of keeping the cold at bay.

He reached the pass and was relieved to find that it was open, as DingXiang's apprentice had said. Strangely enough, once they were between the towering boulders,

Long's *dan tien* began to warm. He halted the horse and looked all around, but saw nothing.

Then he looked up.

A large man dressed head to toe in black dropped a net over Long. The net was ringed with rocks, and it pressed down on him with incredible force. It was difficult for Long to raise his arms, and nearly impossible to raise his head in order to see straight.

GuangZe stamped his hooves nervously, but to his credit stood his ground. Long heard horses' hooves pounding against the rocky ground around a bend ahead, and he fought to free himself. It was no use. The more he struggled, the worse he got tangled in the coarse webbing. He realized that GuangZe's head and legs were unobstructed, so he squeezed his thighs to get the horse moving and steered it back out of the pass, onto the sand.

Long fought gravity, motion, and the ever-shifting sand itself to remain balanced atop GuangZe as his mind raced for a solution. Then he remembered the knife NgGung had given him.

Long managed to wriggle his right hand free of his heavy glove, and he reached behind his sash with two fingers, pulling the small knife from its sheath. It was amazingly sharp, and he made quick work of the webbing. He sliced enough of the net away to free his arms and head, then he resheathed the knife, gripped the reins tightly, and squeezed his thighs together a second time.

GuangZe began to gallop away from the pass, and

whoever was on those other horses had not made it out of the rocks yet. Long thought he was doing well until he heard a strange, drawn-out bellowing, and an arrow zipped past his ear. He glanced over his shoulder to see two black-turbaned archers on horseback clear the pass and come at him from his left flank. A third man cleared the pass and came at him from the right, only this man sat high atop a double-humped *luotuo*. A *camel*!

A second arrow whizzed past Long's head. The archers were on stout, stubby-legged Mongolian horses, which Long knew were relatively slow on normal ground but appeared to be better adapted to running through the sand than GuangZe. GuangZe was now wearing the hoof boots, which had filled with sand and were making it difficult for him to keep in a straight line. The two horsemen were gaining on him.

As for the camel, it was faster still. Its gigantic foot pads spread its weight over a much greater surface than the horses' hooves, and it loped effortlessly after him, complaining loudly as its rider swayed wildly back and forth atop it like Malao atop the mast of Charles' sloop. The camel rider was the one who had dropped the net, and he had a large musket slung across his back. Fortunately, he was moving around so much there was no way that he would be able to unsling it, let alone fire it accurately.

A third arrow zinged past Long's left shoulder, and one of the archers called out, "Stop! These are only warning shots. Give us your horse and we will leave you with your life. Attempt to flee and we will hunt you down!"

Long was not about to stop for anyone. He looked back over his right shoulder and was shocked to see the camel nearly upon him. More surprising, the rider was now standing precariously between the camel's massive humps. The fool was going to jump! Long's eyes widened and he steered GuangZe away from the camel, but it was too late. The camel rider leaped through the air, his shoulder hitting Long square in the back.

Long sailed off his horse into the cold sand; the man landed on one side of him, and Long's water skins slipped off the horse to the other side. The sand was deep here, and it softened Long's fall. He heard the camel scream and caught a glimpse of the beast tumbling end over end. The force of the man's jump must have caused it to stumble.

Long looked over and saw that GuangZe had stopped.

The camel rider shouted beside him, and Long turned to see him staggering to his feet while reaching behind his back for his musket.

"I don't think so," Long hissed. He jumped to his feet and spun toward the man, snapping his fist outward and catching the camel rider on the chin. The man went down hard on his backside and Long leaped at him, but the man was still alert enough to turn away so that Long ended up landing on his back. Long ripped the musket from his attacker's sling and stood, backing away.

"Face me," Long commanded, and he heard a shrill whistle.

Long risked a glance in the direction of the sound and saw that one of the mounted archers had stopped roughly thirty paces from him with his bow drawn and an arrow nocked. The arrow was aimed directly at Long. Long glanced over at GuangZe and saw the second mounted archer take the horse by the reins and begin to lead him toward the first archer. GuangZe went along without a fuss, and Long's heart sank.

As the rush of battle began to wear off, Long noticed something else. There was a pain-filled bellowing in the frigid afternoon air. He looked over at the camel and saw that it was trying to stand, but it kept falling over because one of its front legs no longer worked. The leg dangled limply from its shoulder, obviously broken.

Long lowered the musket. He wasn't sure who he felt sorrier for, the camel or himself.

The camel rider took a step toward him, and Long raised the musket once more. "Keep your distance," he said.

"If you kill me," the camel rider replied, "my friends will kill you."

Long thought back to the standoff the night before. He looked at the man who held GuangZe's reins and saw a scabbardless curved sword dangling at the man's side. Long could clearly make out a large nick in the blade.

Long scowled at the man. "You tried to steal my horse last night! You must be working with Ding-Xiang's apprentice. That is how you knew to ambush me in this particular pass."

The archer with the nicked sword laughed and tied GuangZe's reins to his own horse's saddle. "You should have sold me your horse last night," he said. "Consider yourself fortunate to have lived this long. We would have killed you last night, had DingXiang not arrived. That apprentice of his would sell his own mother for a few taels of silver."

Long heard a noise behind him and turned his head. The camel rider was beginning to circle.

"You have no intentions of letting me live, do you?" Long asked.

"Not anymore," the camel rider replied. "Not knowing the truth about DingXiang's apprentice. The young man is too valuable to us."

Long shook his head. "That is what I thought. I am sorry." He turned the musket toward the archer with the drawn bow and fired.

The barrel erupted with a terrific *BOOM!*, the musket ball flying true. It passed clean through the first archer's chest. The man dropped out of his saddle, but not before releasing his arrow. Long heard a quick buzz rush past him and a sickening *thwack!*

Long turned to see the arrow shaft protruding from the camel rider's right ear. The man fell, stone dead.

GuangZe whinnied and snorted loudly, and Long

heard the second archer curse. Long remembered that Cang had said that GuangZe was afraid of loud noises.

Long spun around to see GuangZe rear up. He pawed at the air with his booted front hooves and shook his head from side to side, trying to free his reins from the second archer's saddle. The saddle rocked wildly, and the man was thrown to the ground.

GuangZe decided to run. The second archer's horse had no choice but to go with him. Both horses disappeared into the pass, tied together.

As Long turned to watch them go, he heard a second *thwack!* and felt white-hot pain sear his side. He glanced down at the right edge of his abdomen, amazed to see a bloody wooden shaft tipped by an arrowhead protruding through the front of his coat. He looked over his right shoulder and saw the arrow's fletching flapping in the breeze behind him.

Long was unsure what to do. The arrow wound hurt more than any of his previous injuries but did not appear to be bleeding too badly.

The second archer reached for his quiver, and Long recovered his wits. He was not about to let that man skewer him again. He reached into his sash and grabbed the knife, ignoring the violent surges of pain that racked his torso. As the archer nocked another arrow, Long snapped his right hand back and then forward, sending the knife through the air and deep into the man's throat.

The second archer dropped, dead as the first archer and the camel rider.

Long was determined to not have his life end here in the desert. He needed to get moving, but he also needed to do something about his new injury. He knew better than to pull the arrow out and open the wound. The arrow was serving as a plug. However, if he was to travel, he had to take care of the long shaft sticking out from either side of him.

While he still had his strength, Long grasped the arrow with both hands and snapped off the arrowhead in front of him. Then he took a deep breath, grasped the fletching, and snapped the tail off the arrow behind him.

Flashes of blinding light exploded behind Long's eyes. He staggered and fell to the sand. He forced himself to roll onto his left side in order to try to lift the right half of his coat and robe to better assess the damage done to his body.

Long managed to lift his jacket and robe up to his waist before he passed out from the pain.

CHAPTER 16

Long woke many hours later and found himself still lying on his left side in the sand, his right hand clenching his jacket and robe. He groaned and sat up in the evening sun.

He looked down at his jacket, and, while it was bloody, he had expected it to be much worse. The pain in his side had subsided significantly as well. He lifted his jacket and robe and saw the broken arrow shaft in the far right side of his abdomen. He felt his back and found that the shaft had passed to the right of his right kidney, just below his rib cage.

He was fortunate. The arrow had missed his vital organs. It had not even cracked a single rib. It was a painful wound, to be sure, and he had bled a fair amount, but he would not die from the injury. He might, however, die from exposure. It was too late to attempt any more travel today, and he needed to find shelter.

Long glanced around and was pleased to at least see the first archer's horse. It had walked over to the rocks and was using them as a shield against the cold wind. Best of all, it did not look like it had any intention of running off like the other two horses had.

Long pushed himself to his feet and staggered toward the stubby Mongolian horse. He remembered the attacker saying the previous night that his horses knew their way to Tunhuang blindfolded. Long hoped this was true. While it would certainly be a shorter journey for him to ride the horse back to DingXiang's outpost, he was determined to complete his goal of meeting with Xie.

Long reached the horse and found it to be quite friendly. He led it to a rock outcropping that provided better protection and secured it. He was about to look for his water skins when he heard a low moan. It did not sound like anything he had ever heard before, and he remembered the camel. It was still alive.

Long frowned, hating what he had to do next. He checked the thief's saddlebag and found the pistol that had been pointed at him the previous night. It was loaded with a single shot, and he used it to put the poor camel out of its misery.

Next he walked over to where he had last seen his water skins, and his heart sank. The containers had all been trampled, their contents emptied.

Averting his eyes from the three dead thieves, Long sighed and looked at the sky. It would be dark sooner than he had realized. Powerless to do anything more, he walked back to the rocks and curled up next to the horse, willing himself to sleep. However, with the darkness came a cold unlike any he had experienced.

The rocks did little to keep the frigid swirling winds at bay, and by the time the moon rose, Long was shivering uncontrollably. He knew that if he did not do something, he would freeze to death. He needed better shelter, but the only thing he could think to use was the camel.

Long stood and stretched his tight muscles as best he could with his injured side before heading over to the carcass. The camel had only been dead a few hours, but it was already as rigid and cold as the stone Long had been lying on. He had heard stories of desperate people who had gutted an animal and slept inside its body cavity to protect themselves from sandstorms or insurmountable winter winds, but there was no way he could bring himself to do that.

This left Long with only one option—skinning the beast. Or at least, skinning a section of it. He doubted he would need the entire hide.

Long reached for the knife in its sheath, then remembered that it was no longer there. He swallowed hard and headed for the fallen second archer. He removed the knife from the man's throat, trying hard not to think about what he had done, and returned to the camel.

He had never skinned an animal before, and the hide was much tougher than he had expected. Working by moonlight made the task even more tedious. It took him nearly an hour to remove an area from the camel's back and sides large enough to wrap himself in. One benefit of all this activity was that he had warmed enough to at least stop shivering. On the other hand, his wound began to drip blood again, sapping his strength.

With the section of hide cut free, Long proceeded to scrape as much fatty tissue as possible from the skin with his knife. Then he carried his heavy camel-hair blanket over to his earlier resting place beside the horse, spread the hide out skin side down upon the rock, and collapsed into it.

The camel hair was dusty, but it was surprisingly soft and thick. He eased over to one end, gripped a corner, and rolled himself into the hide, taking great care to not disturb his wound. Warmer and more secure than he'd thought possible, he closed his eyes and went to sleep.

The sun was high the next day when Long emerged from his camel-hair wrap. He checked the arrow shaft in his side and found that the area was incredibly sore but scabbing over. He was thirsty and began to seriously consider heading back to the outpost. After all, trying to cross a section of desert in two or three days without water could easily mean death. There were also the horse's water needs to consider.

He thought of the Supreme Rule of Three. A person can survive three weeks without food, three days without water, and three minutes without air. The question was, how far did he want to push his luck?

Long remembered pulling the pistol from a saddlebag the day before, but he had not bothered to pay attention to whatever else was inside the bag. He opened it, and to his astonishment found two small water skins tucked beneath a bag of pistol bullets, the man's powder horn, and a coil of rope. He discarded the bullets and powder and raised one of the water skins to his lips.

He drank the entire thing and found that he was still thirsty. He consumed half of the second skin and gave the rest to the horse from his cupped hands.

These small efforts exhausted Long. The wound had definitely weakened him. However, he was feeling better about his chances of success since he had found the water, and he decided to press on toward Tunhuang. He used some of the rope in the saddlebag to secure his camel-hair blanket to the back of the saddle, and he climbed onto the horse and steered it toward the pass. Or, more accurately, it steered him. The horse clearly knew the way.

Long settled into the saddle, leaning back against the plush camel hide. He soon fell asleep. When he woke, it was very late. It was dark and the moon was out. He was so weak now that he was concerned he might fall off the horse and never be heard from again.

Using a section of the remaining rope, Long lashed

himself to the saddle with the camel-hair blanket draped across his shoulders for added warmth. He still wore his jacket, hat, and heavy gloves, but he figured the blanket more than doubled his chances of survival in the bitter nighttime temperatures.

He drifted in and out of consciousness over what he guessed were the next two days, though he could not be sure. He became so dizzy from blood loss and then dehydration, sometimes he could not even tell if it was day or night. Yet this whole time, his horse continued at a steady pace, never stopping.

On what Long thought was probably the third morning since lashing himself to the saddle, he imagined he heard voices and hooves rushing across sand. Without much hope that this was anything more than a hallucination, he raised his weary head.

Long saw two rough-looking young men ride up to him atop Heavenly Horses. They wore black turbans, which led him to believe that they were thieves. He opened his mouth to speak and put up at least a verbal fight, but even his vocal cords had failed him.

The men began to talk with one another in a language he did not understand. Even so, it was clear that they were deciding what they should do with him. One of the men reached over and removed Long's gloves. They were going to steal the clothes right off his back!

The thief started talking excitedly to the other man, and Long realized that they were both staring at his left hand. More specifically, at the scorpion ring Xie had given him. Surely they would steal that, too.

Long was shocked when he was addressed in perfect Mandarin Chinese. "We are so glad to have found you, young dragon!"

Dumbfounded, Long focused all his energy and managed to mouth a single word. "How?"

"A Heavenly Horse arrived in Tunhuang two days ago. It was tied to an old Mongolian horse that appeared to have led it there. Both were riderless, and the Heavenly Horse was wearing hoof boots that had filled with sand. It was clear that something was amiss. When the story was reported to Warlord Xie, he thought of you and sent two hundred pairs of men out into the desert to discover what had happened. No one expected to find you alive, but here you are! You look like you could use a lake's worth of fresh water and several nights by a warm fire."

Long did his best to nod, and the man smiled warmly.

"We will have you in Tunhuang before you know it."

CHAPTER 17

Ying circled the bandits' former stronghold for the hundredth time, as eager to find a bandit as he was to ambush one of Tonglong's elite soldiers. He had important information to give to one group, and equally important information to take from the other. He did not care which encounter happened first. In the end, he was going to get what he wanted, and that was Tonglong's head.

Ying glanced down at Grandmaster's sword, dangling scabbardless from his sash. It glimmered in the moonlight. Its brilliance was likely to give him up to a keen eye, so he had been limiting his patrols here to the nighttime. Even then, he did his best to remain hidden within shadows.

He had come almost a week ago, after ShaoShu had told him about Tonglong's short-term intentions. He needed to warn the bandits, but had no idea how to find them. He decided that if he were Mong, he would have bandit spies patrolling the stronghold's outer reaches in search of information about Tonglong's plans. Find a spy and he could find Mong.

As for Tonglong's elite soldiers, find one of them and, with a little persuasion, he should be able to find their leader, too. He had seen many soldiers, but none had been wearing the red uniforms ShaoShu had told him about. They had all been Commander Woo's men, out on routine patrols, and would not have access to the kind of information Ying desired. As tempted as he was to interrogate a few of them, he had let them all pass. When the time came for one of Tonglong's men—if not Tonglong himself—Ying would be ready.

His grandfather's sword would be ready, too. He had spent hours refurbishing it to its former deadly glory. He had gotten nearly every speck of rust off the blade with the help of abrasive stones and river sand. He had always been good with metal, having spent years helping at Cangzhen Temple's small forge. He had even made his extra-long chain whip himself. He knew good metal when he saw it, and this was the best he had ever held. With additional polishing and a proper whetstone, he could rejuvenate the sword's legendary edge. Even now, it would get the job done.

Ying continued his hunt in the moon shadows of the stronghold. He moved quickly and with purpose.

Before he knew it, the sun had begun to rise, and he found himself on the opposite side of the stronghold lake's sizable perimeter from where he normally hid for the day.

He looked around for a place to hide and spied a thick tract of tall reeds following the shoreline for quite some distance. The ground would be soft and dank in there, but the reeds would be great cover.

Not long after entering the reeds, Ying felt his *dan tien* begin to stir, and he heard what sounded like a dog growling. He had never known soldiers to use dogs, but the bandits might. Dogs would make a powerful first line of defense.

He stopped and was readying Grandmaster's sword for a canine attack when a strange-looking man slipped through the reeds and faced him. The man had huge brown eyes, a big nose, and oversized ears.

The man looked Ying over, then sniffed the air. *Sniff. Sniff.* "What are *you* doing here?" he asked.

"Looking for friends," Ying replied.

The strange-looking man laughed. "*You?* Friends? Ha-ha-ha!"

Ying took a deep breath and reminded himself that he was not there to make enemies with the bandits, for this man was indeed one of Mong's men. His name was Gao, or Dog. Ying had caught glimpses of him in and around the bandit stronghold when the bandits still controlled it.

"I suggest you—" Gao began, but he was interrupted by a tremendous shriek from a line of tall cedar trees bordering the reeds. Ying looked up to see a large white one-eyed macaque glaring down at him. It bared its huge fangs.

This circus is going to attract attention, Ying thought. He looked back at Gao and saw that Gao was unconcerned about the monkey. Gao sniffed the air again.

The white monkey shrieked a second time, and Ying saw Gao tense. Ying fought the urge to look up at the monkey, keeping his eyes fixed on Gao. While an attack from the toothy macaque would be bad, an attack from Gao would be worse.

A soft voice drifted toward Ying from the cedar boughs overhead. "Malao! Can you make that monkey quiet down? The last thing we need is soldiers finding us because of his noise."

"I can try," a small voice replied. "I don't think we need to worry, though. I just heard Gao sniffing. He's in the reeds."

Ying recognized the voices and relaxed. He saw Gao relax, too. That was surely Hok and Malao.

"I thought I smelled your feet, Malao," Gao said in the direction of the voices. "Over here. There is someone you should see."

The treetops began to rustle beyond the white macaque, and Ying saw two figures descend. One swung down on a vine, while the other seemed to float to the ground.

A moment later, Malao broke through the reeds and froze, his eyes locking on Ying's.

The white monkey let out a howl from overhead

and leaped down onto Malao's shoulder. The macaque was huge, weighing nearly as much as Malao, but Malao took the monkey's weight in stride. He did not show the slightest strain as the macaque bared its impressive fangs at Ying, noticeably irritated.

Ying nodded to Malao, but Malao did not acknowledge the greeting. Ying thought Malao might bare his teeth, too, but then Hok stepped into the reeds.

"Ying!" Hok said, sounding genuinely happy to see him. "What are you doing here?"

"I have recent news from ShaoShu," Ying replied. He glanced at Gao, then looked back at Hok. "It concerns the bandits."

Hok's eyes widened. "You saw ShaoShu? How is he?"

"He was fine when I saw him a few days ago at Cangzhen Temple. He is with Tonglong."

"Tonglong arrived at the stronghold several days ago," Gao said. "What news do you have that concerns us?"

"Tonglong knows about the troops you are training," Ying said. "He plans to attack, likely any day now. He has an elite force of ninety-nine men on horseback, plus there are the soldiers in the stronghold. That would be a sizable group. He plans to crush you, and once the remainder of his troops arrive—now tens of thousands strong—he will march upon the Forbidden City in an effort to seize the throne."

Gao nodded. "We knew his plan involved the

Forbidden City, but that he knows about our troops is news to us. We need to take action."

"You need to retreat," Ying said. "Unless you have pistols, muskets, and cannons."

"We have very little in the way of firearms," Hok said. "Unless Charles manages to—"

Gao held up a hand. "Ying does not need to know about our secret resources."

"Charles is no secret to Ying," Hok said. "He and Charles are friends, just as Ying is my friend. We can trust him." She looked at Ying. "As I was saying, we are hoping Charles can find some firearms for us. In the meantime, we train mostly with spears."

Ying spat. "I suppose every little bit helps. Where is your camp? We should warn the others immediately."

"Whoa," Gao said, holding up his hands. "I am not sure you should be shown its location."

Hok glared at Gao. "I just told you that Ying can be trusted. I would bet my life on it."

"You might just have to," Gao said. "Even if he proves trustworthy, there are many within the camp who would love to tear him limb from limb after he helped capture our stronghold."

"I am truly sorry for my actions," Ying said, "and I do not blame you for hating me. However, you once fought against the Emperor, and now it appears you are his ally against Tonglong. Perhaps you can reconsider me, as you have reconsidered him."

Gao scratched one of his large ears. "You raise a good point. Why is it that you want to come to our camp, though? We could just as easily convey this information without you."

Ying nodded toward his grandfather's sword. "I need a whetstone. If you can provide me with one now, I'll be on my way."

"Isn't that Grandmaster's sword?" Gao asked.

"Yes."

"Do you promise to never use it against me or any of our men and women at the camp?"

"I do," Ying said. "The only flesh this blade will cut is Tonglong's."

Gao nodded. "Since Hok says that you can be trusted, you may follow us to the camp. However, I suggest that you remain out of sight. There is no telling how people will react to you. Stay back in the trees, and I will find you the finest sharpening stone we possess." He nodded at Grandmaster's sword. "That blade looks like it deserves it."

Ying followed well behind Gao and Malao, with Hok at his side and the white macaque overhead. Ying and Hok conversed in low voices as they hurried along. Hok told him of her adventures since they had parted company in the south, and Ying gave her a detailed account of his encounter with ShaoShu. By the time their conversation reached the present moment, it was late afternoon.

"Will Fu and Seh be at the camp?" Ying asked.

"They should both be there," Hok replied. "Seh never leaves, and Fu and his father were supposed to return to the camp last night, along with my mother. They were on patrol with us, but their watch ended."

"Are their replacements patrolling the other side of the stronghold?"

Hok shrugged. "The replacements never showed up. That happens sometimes, especially with newer recruits. They get lost or become frightened upon seeing soldiers, and they run off."

Ying frowned. "I wonder if Long will get lost on his way to Tunhuang."

"Long will make it. You of all people should know that."

"What do you mean?"

"You know how tenacious he can be. He is a lot like you."

"I suppose."

Hok shook her head. "No, he truly is a lot like you—in more ways than you are likely to know. In fact, he asked me to share something with you."

"Such as?"

"I am not sure how to tell you."

"Just say it," Ying said.

Hok pursed her lips. "Long is your cousin. Your father and his father were brothers."

"And?"

" 'And?' " Hok repeated. "You knew?"

"No, but it does not surprise me. Long is a dragon, like Grandmaster was. I am a dragon, too. Long and I also look alike. I have never told anyone this, but part of the reason I changed my appearance was so that I would look less like Long."

"Really?"

Ying nodded. "So Grandmaster was Long's grandfather, as well as mine?"

"That is what Grandmaster told him."

"Did Long know how he came to Cangzhen Temple in the first place? I remember he was already there when I arrived, but he was a tiny infant."

"It pains me to tell you this," Hok said, "but apparently your father killed Long's parents."

Ying rubbed his carved forehead. "I guess I believe it. Before I reunited with my mother I would not have, but she has told me stories about what a horrible man my father was. I wish Grandmaster had told me some of it."

"If he had, would you have believed him?"

"Probably not. However, I would have believed that he was my grandfather. As much as I did not like him, I always felt a bond with him. If I had known we were related, I might not have killed him, and we would not be in this situation now."

Ying felt his *dan tien* begin to tingle, and he rubbed his stomach.

"Do you think there is trouble ahead?" Hok whispered.

Ying nodded. Hok rushed on, and Ying followed her. They caught up to Gao and Malao, and Gao raised his nose into the breeze, sniffing loudly. His face twisted, and his big brown eyes filled with fury. "Gunpowder! Someone is loading firearms."

Shots rang out, and the white monkey shrieked above them.

Malao shrieked, too. "The camp is under attack! Fu! Seh! We have to help them!" He raced into the leafless treetops and disappeared, the white macaque leading the way.

Gao and Hok broke into a run.

Ying did his best to keep up with them, but it was no use. Gao dodged between trees and bounded over obstacles with the agility of a wolf, while Hok had always possessed the unnatural ability to glide through the forest faster and more silently than any human Ying had ever seen. Malao was long gone, leaping tree to tree like a rabid monkey.

Ying was able to follow Gao's tracks easily enough, though, and he did not slow his pace until he heard shouting and saw clouds of black smoke. The camp was burning.

Ying came to a small clearing and stopped. What he saw before him was utter chaos. Not only because of the number of firearms, but because of the horses. Close to one hundred soldiers sat atop war stallions, firing pistols and muskets at the bandits and their recruits, who were scurrying about, wielding only spears and swords.

The soldiers were well trained, firing their single-shot weapons in coordinated waves so that one group was always firing while the others reloaded. A few of the recruits were able to connect with their lengthy weapons, but many more were falling to the bullets or being trampled beneath the horses' hooves. It was a massacre in the making.

Ying sank back into what little shadow the leafless trees provided and watched a soldier methodically torching the few bandit tents that were not already ablaze. The bandits were clearly outclassed.

Ying began to circle the clearing, searching for a way to help, and found a handful of bandits doing some significant damage. Ying recognized some of these individuals alongside his former temple siblings. They were well organized and fought in pairs, one adult bandit with one young person. He could not help but admire the way in which they worked together.

Mong, the bandit leader, fought with his back to his son, Seh. Seh was spinning a spear with deadly precision, while Mong fought with his bare hands, pulling soldiers off horses. Hok was with a beautiful woman who Ying assumed was her mother, Bing, or Ice. Both Hok and Bing battled empty-handed, their lightning-fast crane-beak fists dealing with the soldiers unseated by Mong and Seh.

Fu was there, too, fighting back-to-back with a large bandit known as Sanfu. Fu was holding a pair of tiger hook swords, ripping soldiers from their mounts, while Sanfu followed up with mighty swings of a gigantic broadsword. Malao and the white monkey attacked from the trees, the monkey clawing at soldiers' faces while Malao knocked them from their horses with his carved Monkey Stick.

Ying also saw Hung, the bandit known as Bear, whirling a pair of immense war hammers. Hung fought alongside Gao, who brandished no fewer than five pistols. Together they kept a group of relentless soldiers away from a regal-looking man who Ying knew to be the governor of the region.

Gao had apparently run out of loaded weapons, and Ying watched him hurl one of his pistols at a mounted soldier in obvious frustration.

In response to Gao's action, someone called out, "Gao! Over here! I have something for you!"

Ying saw that the speaker was a bandit in tattered clothes sitting atop a magnificent warhorse thirty paces from Gao. The man pulled a pistol from his sash. "It's loaded! Come and get it!"

Gao ran over to the man. Reaching up for the pistol, he said, "Nice horse. Who did you steal it from?"

The man smirked. "No one. Tonglong gave it to me." Then the man aimed the pistol at Gao and fired.

Ying's eyes widened, aghast. He watched as the bullet struck Gao in the chest. Gao coughed up a mouthful of blood, then dropped.

Fu and Sanfu roared in unison, and they raced toward the mounted bandit. Fu shouted, "*You* were supposed to relieve my watch at the stronghold last night! Instead, you led Tonglong here!"

The man laughed and nodded. He pulled another pistol from his sash and aimed it at Fu, but did not get a chance to fire. Hung attacked the man from his blind side. One swing of the mighty hammers crushed the rider's skull.

The monkey shrieked overhead, and Ying looked up to see Malao beside it, pointing with his blood-streaked Monkey Stick toward a wall of smoke across the clearing. "Tonglong is coming!"

"Bandits, retreat!" Mong shouted.

Bandits began to race into the trees from every direction, with mounted soldiers close on their heels. Ying turned toward the smoke and saw a rider barreling forward across the open ground, a line of additional horsemen behind him.

Now what? Ying thought. Grandmaster's sword would be useless against a charge like that.

He tore his chain whip from the pocket in his robe sleeve, and as Tonglong emerged from the smoke, Ying rushed into the clearing and lashed out at the front legs of Tonglong's horse. The extra-long chain wrapped itself around the horse's knees, and the animal went down in a heap. Ying locked eyes with Tonglong as Tonglong sailed forward over the horse's head, and Ying could see the surprise of recognition written across Tonglong's face. Ying knew that Tonglong had thought him to be dead.

Ying watched Tonglong crash headfirst into a stand of saplings at the clearing's edge, their trunks snapping like twigs. Tonglong lay still as his horse skidded and thrashed about, managing to stand and shake the chain whip from its bloody legs.

The riders in Tonglong's wake somehow steered around Tonglong's horse, and Ying thought, *Those men are very, very good riders. Let's find out how skilled they are with weapons.*

As Tonglong's horse hobbled off, Ying snatched his chain whip from the ground and headed for Tonglong.

The soldiers on horseback formed a barrier between Ying and Tonglong's unmoving body. There were ten mounted soldiers in all, and three of them raised their pistols and pointed them in Ying's direction.

Ying did not care. If Tonglong wasn't already dead, Ying would put the final nail in his coffin, regardless of the consequences.

Ying began to swing his chain whip overhead like a lasso, preparing to slice every one of those soldiers to pieces. He had taken two steps toward the line of horsemen when he was knocked violently to the ground. At the same instant, three pistols rang out, their bullets throwing up chunks of earth where he had been standing.

Ying rolled several times and popped to his feet. He was beginning to wrap his chain whip around one hand, ready to smash his attacker with it, when he saw that it was Fu who had tackled him.

Fu scrambled to his feet. "Run, you idiot! This way!" He sprang into a thick stand of pine trees, and two more shots rang out, the bullets striking the soft trunks.

Ying leaped into the evergreens after Fu, landing out of the soldiers' sight. He was about to crawl deeper into the interwoven pine boughs when he heard a familiar voice. He spun around on his stomach and peered into the clearing through a tiny opening in the wall of pine needles.

"What happened?" ShaoShu shouted, emerging from the smoke atop a pony.

The horsemen ignored ShaoShu. Eight of them fanned out across the clearing to guard against a possible counterattack by the bandits, while two riders remained in front of Tonglong's body.

It appeared that ShaoShu was at a loss as to what to do with himself. He steered his pony over to the tree line and began to ride slowly along the clearing's perimeter. As he neared Ying's hiding spot, Ying whispered through the pines, "ShaoShu! It's me, Ying. Find out if Tonglong is still alive."

To his credit, ShaoShu did not bat an eye. He acted as though Ying were not even there and casually turned his pony around, heading back toward the two horsemen.

One of the horsemen scowled at ShaoShu. "Where do you think you are going?"

"I want to check on our leader," ShaoShu said. "To see if he needs help."

"No one could survive a fall like that. We are just protecting his remains in case the bandits return."

"I would hate to be you if he is still alive and he finds out you said that."

The man glowered at ShaoShu, and the second horseman spoke up. "Let the kid take a look. What can it hurt?"

Ying watched as ShaoShu dismounted and hurried over to Tonglong's side. ShaoShu began to fidget about Tonglong's neck, and he suddenly stopped and pointed across the clearing. "Hey!" he said in a worried tone. "I think I see someone in the smoke!"

The two horsemen looked away, and Ying saw ShaoShu slip something into the folds of his robe.

The horsemen looked back at ShaoShu. "What were you pointing at? There's nothing—"

"He's alive!" ShaoShu interrupted, genuine surprise in his voice. "He's breathing!"

The horsemen looked at each other, their eyes wide. "Let's get him away from these flames!" one of them said. They dismounted, and ShaoShu scurried away, hurrying in Ying's direction. When he got to the edge of the clearing, he pretended to trip, stumbling and tumbling into the pines. He stopped next to Ying.

Ying could not help but smirk. "You are insane," he whispered.

"I know," ShaoShu whispered back. He slid one hand into his robe and pulled out a key tied to a thin strand of silk. The key was entwined with dragons. "Take this. It is supposed to open one of the gates or something at the back of the Forbidden City."

Ying took the key and stared into ShaoShu's tiny eyes in disbelief. "I do not know how I will ever be able to repay you."

"Take me with you. Weeks ago I told Tonglong that Hok was dead, but I am sure he saw her fighting here just now. He will kill me."

"Do you think he will live? That was a nasty fall."

Ying's question was answered by a loud groan from Tonglong. Ying peeked back out through the pine boughs. Amazingly, the two horsemen were helping Tonglong to sit up. His head sagged under the weight of his long ponytail braid, but he was clearly conscious and had the use of his arms and legs. He appeared to be fine, and coming around fast.

ShaoShu peeked out, too. "Tonglong is wearing the famous white jade armor beneath his robes. I saw some of the little plates when I took the key."

"That would explain why the branches did not impale him," Ying said.

"We had better get out of here," ShaoShu said, pointing east. "The bandits ran that way."

"Let them run where they may," Ying whispered. "It is Tonglong who we will follow. Now that he knows that I am alive, too, he will not rest until he is deep within the walls of the Forbidden City. Let us hunt him down and paint those walls with his blood."

ShaoShu nodded, and Ying nodded back.

Ying slipped the key into the folds of his robe and backed away through the pines on his hands and knees.

ShaoShu scurried after him.

CHAPTER 19

"How are you feeling?" Xie asked.

"Ridiculous," Long replied.

"I am asking about your health since you arrived five days ago," Xie said. "Not your pride at this moment."

Long sighed. "I am fine, and my wound is healing nicely. I would feel better, however, if your friend stopped treating me like a human pincushion. That arrow through my side was enough, thank you."

Xie's personal tailor buzzed around Long like a busy bee, measuring and pinning sections of illegal yellow silk around Long's body. Only the Emperor was allowed to wear yellow.

Long shook his head. Why had he agreed to this charade?

Xie had a plan to deal with Tonglong, and it was as elaborate as it was simple. Xie had formally taken control of his father's troops, and as the Western Warlord he had commanded his generals to pull troops from the farthest reaches of their region to meet with the bandits outside the Forbidden City as Mong had suggested. However, what if Mong's best guess was incorrect and Tonglong showed up at the Forbidden City several weeks before the New Year? Xie was convinced that they needed to take additional action.

Xie realized that since no one was exactly sure where the Emperor was, no one would question it if the Emperor happened to return to the Forbidden City. Meaning, if someone *pretended* to be the Emperor, that person would not be questioned. Especially if he looked like the Emperor and was accompanied by Xie, who everyone recognized as the Emperor's bodyguard and most people feared. Long was about the Emperor's size and would be given a wide berth whenever Xie was around, which would be all of the time.

Thankfully, today's robe fitting would be the last, and they would be on their way by the end of the day. In order to keep things as authentic as possible, they would transport Long in royal style, complete with armed guards and a sedan chair. Long was looking forward to it.

Xie and Long had discussed the possibility that Tonglong might find out about the procession and attack them, but Xie thought that the chance was very slight. They would be traveling through the vast open spaces of the Western and Northern armies' regions, and Tonglong would not be caught within a hundred *li* of them without a full complement of thousands of troops.

After a quiet lunch, they set off. Long would have thought there might be a problem with the secrecy of their mission being compromised because of all the people in Tunhuang who knew of the plan, but Xie assured him that nothing would be jeopardized. Everyone within Xie's inner circle had been loyal to Xie's father, and they were all eager to see Tonglong pay.

Long began the journey in the sedan chair with Xie at his side atop a Heavenly Horse, as was protocol. The sedan chair had long poles stretching in front of and behind it for men to hoist upon their shoulders; this one, however, had been modified so that horses could carry it as well. They were in a hurry, and the horses could walk twice as fast as humans. They could also run, if necessary.

The sedan chair had blinds that could open, and Long and Xie talked through them for hours. Xie explained that there was something called the Silk Road, which was a network of loose trails that connected China with the West. Goods were transported in both directions over this "road," and Tunhuang was one of the major stops. Much of the road was hostile desert, so cities like Tunhuang were important points for the buying and selling of supplies for weary travelers. Trade also occurred here, and it was this trade that made Tunhuang one of the richest cities in the world.

As they approached the outskirts of the city, Long

saw a great wall. In fact, Xie told him, it was *the* Great Wall, which was known by many different names. This wall began thousands of *li* away in China's southeast, and ended here in Tunhuang in the northwest. The wall had been built in sections over the course of more than two thousand years, and was created to keep marauding "outsiders" like Mongolians from getting into China.

Long was surprised when they reached the wall and Xie told him that they would travel to the gates of Peking—the city in which the Forbidden City was located—on top of the wall. Long's sedan chair was carried up a gigantic stone staircase, and once they reached the top he found the wall to be massive both in height and thickness. It was so wide across the top that several horsemen could ride beside one another down its entire length.

They began their march east, and Long soon learned that in many ways, the wall was as much for communication as it was for protection. Not only could horses race across it to deliver messages, signal fire and drum stations were positioned at regular intervals to allow soldiers to pass information along with amazing speed.

Long also saw that watchtowers had been built every thousand paces along the wall's top, and that there were four soldiers in each tower at all times, scanning the horizon. The towers were designed with special windows to make it easy for archers to shoot out of but difficult for enemy archers to shoot arrows into. Additionally, many of the watchtowers in high-trouble areas were equipped with cauldrons of boiling oil to pour down upon enemy combatants attempting to scale the wall.

It seemed every possible precaution had been taken into account when building the wall. Long wondered how many of these design ideas had made their way into the Forbidden City. If Tonglong ever made it there, they were going to need all the help they could get.

CHAPTER 20

ShaoShu crossed the frosty hillside in the night, his cupped hands filled with cold boiled dumplings. He reached the mouth of a small cave and snuck past the two sleeping guards like a rodent slipping past napping felines. If Tonglong ever found out that these soldiers had slept on the job, he would eat their livers for breakfast.

ShaoShu crept to the back of the cave, over to the stinking, battered pig crate. He knocked lightly on its side. "Emperor, it's me, ShaoShu. Are you awake, sir?"

A weary voice groaned within the crate. "Little Mouse, what are you doing here? I was told you ran off."

"I did run off—with Ying, after the battle with the bandits. However, we have been following Tonglong ever since. We've been spying on him and his men, and I've been swiping food, too. I've brought you some. Here it comes."

ShaoShu carefully dropped seven dumplings through one of the crate's airholes.

"Thank you," the Emperor said.

"You are most welcome. How are you doing?"

"Much better whenever you sneak food to me. I have missed you. If I should make it out of here alive, you will be rewarded handsomely."

"I only want to spend time with my friends."

"Are you referring to the young Cangzhen monks you have told me about?"

"Yes."

"That is most admirable of you. Do you include Ying among this lot?"

"Yes, sir."

"I still find it difficult to believe that Ying is attempting to help me," the Emperor said.

"It's true," ShaoShu replied. "In fact, he is the reason you are heading to the Forbidden City so far ahead of schedule."

"What do you mean?"

"Ying having attacked Tonglong is driving Tonglong crazy. Literally. I have watched him stomp around camp, ranting and raving to himself about Ying coming back from the grave to try to kill him. I think Ying's attack made him realize that he could die anytime. He was going to wait for all of his troops to arrive at the stronghold before marching to the Forbidden City, but as you can see you are already on the way."

"How long before we get there?"

"The soldiers say about a week."

"How many men does he have again?"

"Some died in the attack against the bandits, but he still has about eighty elite soldiers, plus their horses."

"There are three thousand highly skilled imperial soldiers within the Forbidden City. Tonglong does not stand a chance."

"They keep calling this a 'diplomatic mission,'" ShaoShu said. "Tonglong's men say there will be no bloodshed because of who Tonglong bribed."

"Did they mention any names?"

"Just one, but they say this person is really important—Wuya, or Crow."

"Wuya?" the Emperor asked. "Are you certain?"

"Yes, sir."

"Then we are indeed doomed. Wuya is the head of security for the entire Forbidden City. All three thousand soldiers report to him."

"Uh-oh," ShaoShu said.

"Uh-oh, indeed. To think, I fully trusted Wuya. Apparently another of my many mistakes. When are Tonglong's main forces supposed to arrive?"

"I heard the soldiers say that local squadrons are already arriving at the stronghold, but the troops from the south and east are not supposed to be here for at least another few weeks."

"That is good news. Is there anything else you can tell me?"

"Well, there is the key that I stole from Tonglong and gave to Ying."

"A key?"

"Yes, sir," ShaoShu said. "Tonglong had a key that he claimed opened a back gate or door to the Forbidden City, he wasn't sure which. Just before I ran off, I stole the key and gave it to Ying."

"Do you know where Tonglong got the key?"

"His father, sir."

"What does it look like? A normal key?"

"No, it is entwined with dragons."

"This is *great* news," the Emperor said. "I knew Tonglong's father. If the key is what I think it is, we just might have a chance. That is to say, Ying will get another chance at Tonglong. Now, listen carefully...."

Seh sat at the meeting table inside the secret room above the kitchen at the Jade Phoenix. He and the bandits had only been in Kaifeng a few hours, but the proprietor, Yuen, had told them that rumors were flying thanks to propaganda from Tonglong. She said that locals were saying Tonglong's elite force had killed the bandits, crushing their so-called Resistance.

Seh hated to admit it, but the propaganda was more or less accurate.

Around the table with Seh sat Mong, Hung, Bing, Sanfu, and the Governor; plus Fu, Malao, and Hok. The mood was somber. They were deep in conversation, determining their next course of action.

The Governor cleared his throat and looked at

Mong. "I don't know how to say this, but our best next step may be surrender."

"Never!" Fu growled, slamming his fist on the table.

"We have to be realistic," the Governor said. "No one has worked harder for the autonomy of this region than I have, and no one knows better than I what is at stake. If we had the means to fight, that would be a different story. However, what we have just seen all too clearly is that a volunteer army of well-intentioned men cannot compete against those armed with pistols and muskets."

"We killed some of them," Fu said.

"We killed about twenty horsemen, compared with more than a hundred bandits lost," the Governor said. "That ratio is unacceptable. It will not change significantly unless we have firearms—"

"Did someone say firearms?" a voice called out from the opposite side of the meeting room's trapdoor.

Seh did not recognize the voice right away, but Fu, Hok, and Malao did.

"Charles!" Malao squealed. He jumped out of his chair and pulled the trapdoor open, dropping a rope ladder down into the kitchen. A moment later, Charles' head popped up through the trapdoor.

"I came to ask Yuen where to find you, and here you are!" Charles said. "This must be a sign. I have news."

"Please tell us that your pirate friends are on the way," Malao said. "We could really use the help. Besides, I *love* boat rides." He giggled.

Charles shook his head. "My news is not *that* good. In my quest to find my countrymen, I sailed all the way to the sea before I learned that Tonglong has positioned warships up and down the seacoast. I could not attempt to travel by that route. The Grand Canal turned out to be out of the question, too. There are soldiers everywhere."

"So, what is your good news, then?" Hok asked.

"I sailed back up the Yellow River to Jinan and went to see HukJee, the black market dealer. He has realized that Tonglong as Emperor would be bad for his business, so he offered to help. He will give us firearms."

"Yes!" Fu said.

Mong shook his head. "Not so fast, Fu. Charles, what quantities are we talking about, and what is the timing?"

"HukJee said that he could get two hundred pistols and one hundred muskets to Jinan in five days. He might be able to secure a few cannons, too, plus black powder and shot. I could make a run to Jinan and pick up whatever my sloop can carry, then proceed to the Forbidden City. There is a long canal that links the Forbidden City and the Yellow River. We could meet somewhere along there."

"That is a great idea, Charles," Mong said. "You are going to need help, though. Fu, Malao, Hok, and Seh—how do you feel about traveling with Charles? I think the lot of you could adequately protect a shipment as precious as this."

"All right!" Malao squealed. "A boat ride!"

Charles' face grew grave, and he turned to Malao.

THE

F
I
V
E

A
N
C
E
S
T
O
R
S

"Firearms are dangerous business, my little friend. They need to be taken seriously."

Malao lowered his eyes. "Sorry."

Seh watched Fu and Hok nod solemnly. He nodded, too.

"Thank you," Charles said to them, and he turned to Mong. "I would be honored if my friends could accompany me as crew, and I will teach them to fire what we carry. We will arrive as more than just a transport vessel. We will be a full-blown man-o-war."

"Thank you," Mong replied. "I know this is not your battle to fight, as you come from another land."

Charles looked at each of them, then he bowed to Mong. "It is my battle, sir. You are my friends. I will not let you down."

172

Long spent nearly a week traveling with Xie and the phony imperial caravan atop the Great Wall before they reached the enormous gate at the western edge of the city of Peking. He had learned that the Forbidden City was a walled compound located within these city limits, and soon found his sedan chair being carried down a massive staircase into a gathering crowd.

Word had quickly spread to the city dwellers from the soldiers monitoring the wall's signal fires that the Emperor's caravan was headed their way. The news circulated much faster than the caravan could travel, and by the time Long reached the main gates of the Forbidden City several hours later, he had witnessed thousands upon thousands of people pushing and shoving one another, trying to catch a glimpse of their imperial ruler's sedan chair. Long had never seen anything like either the crowds or the Forbidden City itself.

Outside the largest, most imposing gate he could have imagined, Long heard a gong sound, and the excited crowd fell deathly silent. The Forbidden City's main gate slowly opened, and a wave of people began to push back from it. Soldiers on horseback soon flooded out, driving the crowds back farther still while forming a river of open space through which Long's caravan could pass untouched.

Soldiers saluted and more gongs began to ring out, and Xie poked his head into the sedan chair, unable to suppress his smile. "All this is for you, my friend," he said. "What do you think?"

"I honestly have no idea what to think," Long replied, filled with awe. "Has this ever happened before?"

Xie laughed. "Every single time he enters or leaves. The current Emperor is unusual in that he enjoys traveling, which is a big part of the reason he was captured. Most emperors and empresses rarely left the Forbidden City. As you will see, there really is no need. We are about to enter, so slip your hood over your head and remain silent. No one is allowed to look at you, but it is better to be safe."

Long nodded that he understood, and he sat back to enjoy the tour.

The first thing they came to was a wide moat. They crossed it via a beautiful bridge, then headed through the largest pair of doors Long had ever seen. This "gate" was so tall that he could not even guess at its height, and it was wide enough for several horses to pass through side by side. The gate doors were a marvel of engineering, and nearly as ornate as the bridge had been.

Once they were through, the gate doors closed behind them, and Long noticed a different set of gate doors ahead. On either side of them were sheer walls topped with armed soldiers. Someone sounded a gong, and the second set of doors began to open. They passed through these doors, only to find themselves facing yet another set, with more soldiers along the tops of the side walls. Long whispered out of his window to Xie, "How many of these gates are there?"

"The Forbidden City is cities within cities," Xie replied. "There are walls within walls, and gates within gates. The gates will soon grow progressively farther apart and you will see more and more buildings within each section, but to answer your question there are seven or so gates between the entrance and your palace, depending upon what you consider a gate. The section in which you will live is the most secure area in all China."

"It is going to take all day to get there," Long said with a sigh.

"Hours," Xie replied. "Protocol requires you to

meet with your advisors. There are different advisors for different subjects, and they all occupy different sections of the Forbidden City. Upon arrival, the Emperor must meet with each and every one. The good news is, you do not have to get out of the sedan chair, and they are even forbidden to look directly at you. You will not even need to talk, just listen to what they have to report. The bad news is, we will not be eating supper until midnight."

By the time Long arrived at "his" personal dining hall and dinner was served, it was indeed midnight and he was almost too tired to eat. His head hurt from listening to all the things the Emperor had to deal with. How could one man be responsible for so many details and decisions? There were advisors for everything from foreign trade to national taxation to daily menus for the Emperor's four hundred personal servants. It was mind-boggling. He had a new respect for the Emperor.

"Had enough for one day?" Xie asked.

Long pushed his hood back and rubbed his forehead. "Please do not even joke about that. I don't think I could have taken another meeting or advisor."

"I am sorry to tell you, then, that we have one more meeting. You still have not met the head of security, my best childhood friend, Wuya."

"His name is Crow? Was he ever a warrior monk?"

"No. Like me, he just happens to have a name from nature. Our families have a long history of friendship, and naming children in this manner is a unique habit we share."

There was a knock at the door, and Long quickly flipped up his hood.

A servant stepped into the room and bowed toward Xie. "Security Chief Wuya is here."

"Show him in," Xie said, and he turned to Long and whispered, "Let us see how quickly he notices that you are not the Emperor."

Long nodded and sat very straight, as though he were royalty. He adjusted the hood down well over his face and folded his hands within his long yellow robe sleeves.

Wuya entered the room, and Long saw how well his name suited him. He was tall and thin, with shiny black hair and a large, beaked nose. He stopped several paces from Long and bowed, staring straight at him.

Long grew uncomfortable. Every other advisor had followed tradition and only glanced at him indirectly. This man was scrutinizing him, for some reason.

"Welcome back, Your Eminence," Wuya said.

Long nodded.

"I trust your trip was satisfactory?"

Long nodded again.

"I understand that your caravan approached Peking from the west. Forgive my saying so, Sire, but that is odd. You were expected from the south. You were also expected to be traveling with our new Southern Warlord, Tonglong. Is everything fine? Do I have reason to be alarmed?"

Long shook his head.

Wuya's beady black eyes narrowed. "Which is it,

Sire? Are you shaking your head in response to my first question, or my second?"

Long did not know what to do. He had not spoken all night, knowing that doing so would give him up as an impostor.

Xie clamped a hand on Wuya's thin shoulder. "Wuya, old friend, we need to talk."

Wuya shrugged Xie's hand away. "I am speaking with *the Emperor*. You and I will talk soon enough." He grabbed a small key ring tied to his sash and turned to Long. With an impressively quick flick of his wrist, Wuya flung the keys at Long's face. Long barely had time to catch them before they struck his mouth.

Wuya squawked and pointed at Long, but spoke to Xie. "I *knew* it! Those are the hands of a boy, not a man. Remove your hood."

Long did as he was told.

"Who are you?" Wuya asked.

"It is a long story," Xie replied, looking suspiciously at Wuya. "Before I answer your question, though, I have one for you. You seem to have known from the moment you walked in here that this was not the Emperor. How?"

"You enter the Forbidden City with a child posing as the Emperor, and you want to question *me* about *my* suspicions? I am the head of security. It is my job to be suspicious. If you detected more suspicion than normal in this case, it was obviously warranted. Now tell me, who is he? What are you up to?"

"Have a seat, and I will tell you all about it. There is no need to be rude."

"I will not have a seat!" Wuya said. "Where is the Emperor?"

"He has been kidnapped," Xie replied.

"Kidnapped? By whom?"

"Tonglong."

"The Emperor is traveling under Tonglong's protection. There has been no kidnapping."

Xie shook his head. "The Emperor is being held against his will and, last I saw, was being loaded into a pig crate."

Wuya clenched his teeth. "Why would Tonglong do that?"

"He is power-hungry."

Wuya's tiny eyes blazed with fury. "Of course Tonglong is power-hungry. He is now the Southern Warlord. A person does not get to that level of leadership *without* being power-hungry. One might accuse you of having the same tendencies, Xie, seeing how you are now the Western Warlord."

"Tonglong is different altogether from me, and you know it. I do not appreciate your implications."

"What you do or do not appreciate means nothing," Wuya said. "The security of our country means everything. Let us assume for a moment that Tonglong *was* up to something. You decided on your own that the solution to the problem was to put an impostor on the throne? How dare you! What you are doing amounts to treason."

"How dare *you* speak to me in this manner?!" Xie replied in a menacing tone. "It is only out of respect for our past that I do not tear your head from your bony shoulders this instant. Tonglong is gathering troops. He claims to be doing so with the Emperor's blessing. Why would the Emperor bless that? Think about it. Listen to me."

"No, *you* listen to *me*. I respect our history, and I respect your position as the Western Warlord. More than anything, I respect the fact that you recently lost your father under circumstances that I myself find dubious. However, we are in the Forbidden City. You have no power here. *I* am the head of security. You have put me in a compromising position without consulting me first. If anyone finds out about this game of yours, *I* will be executed." He turned and glared at Long. "You never told me who you are. You look familiar."

"My name is Long," Long replied, "but you may know me as Golden Dragon."

"Of course," Wuya said. "The newest Fight Club Grand Champion. Has anyone else seen your hands tonight?"

"No."

"If a single person suspects anything," Wuya said, "the whole nation could be sent into a panic. I would have no choice but to kill you. I should just kill you now and save myself a world of potential trouble. I suggest you leave immediately, Long. Leave your blasphemous yellow robes here, too."

"He is not going anywhere," Xie said. "We need everyone to continue to think that the Emperor is now inside the Forbidden City and in control. When Tonglong arrives to try to seize the throne—"

"Enough of this Tonglong nonsense!" Wuya said. "Take Long and leave immediately. I will not be held responsible for his safety, or yours."

"I will take full responsibility for both of our lives," Xie said, "but we will not leave on your terms. We will leave when *I* deem it is time."

"Before sundown tomorrow, then," Wuya said. "No later. And do not leave this room."

"Tomorrow evening is fine, but I was planning on him staying in my quarters tonight."

"No. Too many people have seen him. He must stay in the Emperor's suite."

"Then I will stay with him," Xie said, "on the floor by the door."

"You will do no such thing. Never once did you do that with the Emperor. We must do nothing out of the ordinary."

"I have spent many nights outside the Emperor's door."

"Outside the door is acceptable. Inside is not. While you eat dinner, I will secure the room and instruct my men to steer clear of it while you are here. You have broken my confidence, Xie, and I must do what is required of me to protect my interests, as well as the interests of the entire nation."

Before Xie had a chance to say another word, Wuya stormed off.

CHAPTER 23

Long lay in the Emperor's private suite, exhausted but unable to sleep. What was he thinking, coming here and pretending to be the most powerful person under the sun? Wuya was right. This was nonsense. He should have been more concerned about what it could mean for the country, not to mention his own safety and the safety of Xie. He was glad to be leaving tomorrow.

Long closed his eyes and tried to sleep once more. His eyelids had no sooner come together when his *dan tien* began to tingle. At first he thought it was just his overactive mind affecting his body, but he listened intently and soon heard someone coming. But who? And more importantly, why?

Xie had told Long that he would stay outside his door all night. The room was huge, and the strange bed in which Long lay was at its very center. It was difficult to sense anything outside the door from this distance, and it was nearly impossible to see. The room had several windows, but they were set high in the walls and their shutters had been closed for the night, allowing only a small amount of moonlight to peek through.

So where were the sounds coming from?

Long rolled onto his right side and faced the door, concentrating. In the room's darkness, his hearing was his most useful sense. He identified the faintest of clicks as a lock turned, and a barely audible creak as a door swung open. The odd thing was, the sound came from his left—from within the room.

Someone entered. Long felt angry energy seeping from the intruder's pores like sweat.

Long decided to feign sleep. He turned silently flat onto his back, closed his eyelids to slivers, and steadied his breathing. If someone was coming to kill him, they would likely attack his head. As long as he continued to focus in front of his face—

There was a rustle of silk, and Long struck. He rolled out of the bed, swinging his right leg up and around in a powerful arc. He felt his right shin slam into the intruder's body and heard a muffled "Umf!"

Long sprang to his feet, ignoring the pain that erupted from the healing wound in his side. He thrust his hands in the direction of the cry and found the intruder's chest. He kept his fists pressed against the man's body, sliding his hands up and outward until he found the intruder's armpits and the extremely sensitive pressure points where the man's chest muscles connected with his upper arms. Long sank his fingers deep into the pressure points on both sides, and the man cursed, writhing with pain.

Long heard a metallic clatter on the floor and guessed it was a sword. He released the intruder and bent down to grab the object. His hands brushed across an ornate sword handle, and he picked up the sword. It felt oddly familiar.

The intruder hissed like a dragon, and Long could hardly believe his ears. He knew that tone, as well as the sword! He said, "Ying! Stand down! It's me, Long."

The door to the private suite burst open, and Xie rushed in carrying an oil lamp. "Long, I—"

Xie froze, and his eyes followed Ying's gaze toward a section of wood-paneled wall that harbored a secret door. The door was open, and a flame flickered beyond it, growing brighter.

Wuya stepped through the secret doorway, into the Emperor's private suite. "What is going on here?" he demanded.

Xie's face hardened. "I might ask the same question of you." He turned and glared at Ying. "And you as well."

Ying looked from Wuya to Xie and finally to Long. "I believe that I am the most confused of all."

Long looked at the sword in his hand, and he turned to Ying. "You go first. How did you get here? Where did you get Grandmaster's sword?"

"I retrieved the sword from Cangzhen Temple," Ying replied. "I refurbished it in order to kill Tonglong. That is why I am here. Why are you here?"

"You are in no position to question Long or anyone else," Xie interrupted. "How did you know about the secret passageway?"

"A little mouse told me," Ying replied.

"ShaoShu?" Long asked.

Ying nodded. "He traveled here with me, though he is still outside the walls somewhere."

"How did ShaoShu find out?" Xie asked.

"The Emperor."

"He is still alive?" Wuya asked.

Ying nodded.

"How did you get the suite door open?" Xie asked.

"I have a key," Ying replied.

"Where did you get it?"

"ShaoShu stole it from Tonglong."

"You say this ShaoShu stole a Forbidden City key from *Tonglong*?" Wuya asked.

"Wuya, why are you so interested in Tonglong?" Xie asked. "And what were *you* doing coming into Long's suite through the secret passageway? I can only assume you intended to cause Long harm."

Wuya scoffed. "Where I choose to go is none of your business. What are *you* doing here? I ordered you to remain outside of the suite."

"I entered because I heard a scuffle. Truth be told, I was going to enter anyway. I have important news."

"News?" Long asked.

Xie nodded. "Tonglong has arrived."

Long saw Wuya's black eyes sparkle in the light of his oil lamp. "Tonglong?" Wuya asked. "Are you sure?"

"I am certain," Xie said. "I climbed one of the turrets and saw his small army of horsemen myself. They are standing outside the main gate."

"Tonglong is here, without question," Ying said. "ShaoShu and I followed him long enough to know that this was his destination."

Wuya scrambled for the suite's main door. "All three of you, remain here until I return. I have men guarding the secret passageway, the main suite door, and even the windows. Attempt to flee, and you will be shot."

CHAPTER 24

ShaoShu lay hidden beneath a tiny evergreen shrub next to the Forbidden City's moat, trying his best not to be discovered by Tonglong, who stood nearby. ShaoShu was soaking wet and shivering with cold, having swum here in the moat after leaving Ying at the Emperor's secret passageway entrance.

ShaoShu shook the water from his ears and stared at Tonglong silhouetted in the moonlight. It was clear that Tonglong had lost his mind. He stood just outside the open main gate, facing several hundred armed Forbidden City soldiers who were positioned inside. The soldiers were not allowed to set foot outside the gate's threshold, and Tonglong was not being allowed in. It was a standoff.

The Forbidden City soldiers were well armed, but so were Tonglong's remaining elite horsemen, lined up behind him. ShaoShu would give either group an equal chance of success if things escalated into a battle, though there were thousands more soldiers within the Forbidden City who could be called into action to effectively crush Tonglong if someone were to give the order.

ShaoShu heard Tonglong argue that he had arranged to meet Wuya somewhere outside the Forbidden City. However, Wuya had not shown up. Now Tonglong was demanding to be allowed inside to find him. Tonglong was wearing the ceremonial white jade armor traditionally reserved for China's rightful ruler, and holding a white jade sword of similar significance. He glowed like a beacon in the bright moonlight, and seemed to think that his outfit should make the Forbidden City forces bow at his feet.

It did not.

"Do you know who I am?" Tonglong demanded.

"We do, sir," replied the Forbidden City's front gate battalion leader. "However, Xie has issued orders to deny you and your horsemen entry. Only Wuya can override those orders, and he is not available right now."

"Xie!" Tonglong said. "What is *he* doing here?"

"He lives here, sir."

Tonglong frowned. "I *know* that. When did he arrive?"

"I am not at liberty to say, sir."

"When was the last time you saw Wuya?"

"No one has seen him for more than an hour, sir. But I have left word and can assure you that the moment he makes himself available, he will come directly here. The Emperor could override Xie's orders, too, of course, but he has retreated to his palace suite and is likely asleep."

"The Emperor is with me, you fool!"

The battalion leader shook his head. "No, sir. The Emperor arrived hours ago. I saw him with my own eyes. He was rumored to be with you, but that was surely just a ploy to confuse potential enemies. There is no need to continue the facade, sir."

"Foolish man!" Tonglong barked. "Find Wuya or let me in. Now!"

"Sir, I do not report to you. You have no authority over me as long as I am within the Forbidden City."

"Then we will have to do something about that, won't we?" Tonglong dropped the jade sword and rushed toward the battalion leader, crossing the Forbidden City's threshold.

The battalion leader's eyes widened in surprise and he took a step back, but Tonglong closed the gap with astonishing speed. He bent his arms and raised his elbows straight out in front of himself, forming fists with both hands. Then he extended his index fingers and pointed them straight down at the ground.

Tonglong's forearms and hands now looked just like the forearms and claws of a praying mantis. His right hand shot out behind the battalion leader's neck, and he used his hooklike fist to pull the man's face toward him. At the same time, his left hooklike fist took hold of the man's chin.

Tonglong leaped back through the Forbidden City's gate, dragging the stumbling battalion leader with him. He shoved the man's chin around with a vicious twisting motion, and the battalion leader's neck snapped.

Tonglong hurled the lifeless body to the ground.

The entire battalion of Forbidden City soldiers raised their muskets, aiming them at Tonglong.

Tonglong picked up the jade sword and glared back along the ranks. "I will pull *each* of you out here, one at a time, unless someone brings Wuya to me this instant. I—"

"Front Gate Battalion, stand down!" a sharp voice interrupted from overhead.

ShaoShu looked up to see a man with black hair and a beaked nose striding confidently along the top of the wall, carrying a large oil lamp. It had to be Wuya. He looked just like a crow.

Wuya's head disappeared and, several moments later, he walked through the main gate and glanced down at the dead battalion leader, then looked at Tonglong.

"I heard some of your argument as I approached," Wuya said. "My apologies. The men were acting on orders from someone else. I was attending to urgent matters." He lowered his voice, and ShaoShu strained to listen. "I believe that you will find my time well spent."

"Do these matters involve Xie and the Emperor?" Tonglong whispered.

"They do."

"Is the Emperor here?"

"You know very well where he is. I see that you have brought a sword for me. Thank you. Did you bring the crate?"

"This is *my* jade sword," Tonglong said, his voice still barely more than a whisper. "You will receive yours when you deliver the seals. I have urgent documents to draft and circulate. The crate is here, but it is no concern of yours."

"I am afraid the crate's contents are essential for locating the seals," Wuya replied. "Have your men bring it to the gate, and my soldiers will carry it inside."

"My men are more than qualified to carry the crate."

"No," Wuya said, his voice low. "Until our deal is finalized, your men will wait outside the gate. All of them. The only soldiers allowed inside are Forbidden City soldiers sworn to protect the Emperor."

"My men are sworn to protect *me*," Tonglong said. "That should mean something to you, considering our agreement up to this point. I will not enter alone, and I will not enter unarmed. Neither will my men."

Wuya paused, as if contemplating something. He sighed loudly enough for ShaoShu to hear. "I will make an exception this time."

Wuya raised his voice for all to hear. "You may

bring four men with you to carry the crate. No more. All of you may be armed."

Tonglong nodded.

"Welcome to the Forbidden City," Wuya said.

ShaoShu watched as Tonglong shouted orders and four soldiers, each with a musket slung across his back, picked up the crate ShaoShu knew contained the Emperor. The men followed Tonglong and Wuya across the Forbidden City's threshold, and the enormous gates began to close.

There was no point in ShaoShu hiding there any longer. He needed to give Ying an update. With everyone's eyes still fixed on the closing gate, ShaoShu slipped out of the shrub, back into the moat.

Seh stood on the deck of Charles' sloop in the moonlight, scanning the canal's shoreline for signs of movement. He saw nothing. Neither did Charles, Hok, Malao, or even Fu, with his extraordinary low-light vision.

"Are you sure *this* canal goes all the way to the Forbidden City?" Seh asked. "We have been on it for quite some time and have not seen any sign of the bandits."

"Positive," Charles said. "This is the canal that connects the Forbidden City's moat with the Yellow River. It is the main route over which goods are transported to the Forbidden City from all over the country. I cannot wait to unload *our* cargo there. HukJee really came through for us."

"You can say that again," Seh replied, glancing about at the wooden crates filled with muskets, pistols, and ammunition, not to mention the three small cannons and numerous oak barrels filled with black powder. "Will we be able to sail right up to the gates?"

"No. There are bridges over the moat that we will not be able to sail under because of the height of my mast. Cargo is usually off-loaded to horse-drawn carts at the first bridge. However, that bridge is within shooting distance of the main gate."

"Do you think we will go all the way to the Forbidden City without meeting the bandits?" Hok asked.

"It is possible they went on to the Forbidden City without us," Charles said. "Or maybe they have been delayed and are behind schedule. I am certain that tonight is the night we were supposed to rendezvous."

"I wonder if Tonglong has made it to the Forbidden City yet," Seh said. "If he has—"

"There!" Fu interrupted from the bow. "I see a bridge coming up, and I can just make out a very tall wall beyond it."

"I see it, too!" Malao called down from the very top of the mast, Charles' spyglass in his hands. "And there's the main gate. There are a bunch of horsemen in front of it."

"Bandits?" Seh asked.

"No," Malao replied. "Tonglong's men. They are all wearing red uniforms. Wait, some of them are going inside! Let's blast them!"

"Not so fast," Charles said from the helm. "We need to get closer to be within firing range. We also need to make sure those are Tonglong's men, and not the bandits."

"It's them, all right," Fu said. "Unless Mong, Hung, Sanfu, NgGung, and Bing made seventy new friends who all have horses and like to wear red."

"You can see all that?" Charles asked. "You are not human, Fu."

Fu growled.

"Is it possible to go faster?" Hok asked.

"This is the best we can do," Charles replied. "We cannot risk raising any more sail in this relatively narrow canal, and rowing will do little more than make a lot of noise. They will see us soon enough as it is. Unless you want to turn around—"

"Never!" Fu said. "We will fight."

"Mong said that the bandits could fight Tonglong's army right in front of the Forbidden City gates for days and the imperial army would not get involved," Charles said. "They have sworn an oath to not step foot outside the walls. Do you think this is true?"

"There is only one way to find out," Seh answered.

"They are closing the giant gate!" Malao called down. "Five of Tonglong's men entered without their horses. Four were carrying a big crate."

"Malao," Charles said, "how far do you think we are from them?"

"Based on our practice shots along the Yellow River, I think Fu could hit them with his cannon."

"Did you hear that, Fu?" Charles asked. "Battle stations, everyone!"

Fu remained at the bow and began to load his cannon with black powder and a ball the size of a large peach. Seh and Hok raced to the stern, where Hok set to lighting several lengths of slow match fuse with a piece of flint and steel, while Seh began to load two cannons that were slightly smaller than Fu's. Malao raced down the mast, pulled several loaded pistols from a large wooden box on deck, slipped the pistols behind his wide sash, and scurried back up to the very top of the rigging.

Charles remained at the helm.

Hok glided to the front of the boat and handed Fu a burning piece of slow match, then she ran to the stern and gave Seh one, too. Seh watched as Hok went back to the center of the boat and quickly loaded several muskets, laying them out along the deck in front of her. She shouldered one, and Charles said, "Malao, furl the sail! Everyone else, fire at will!"

Seh saw Malao scurry along the rigging, tying down the mainsail with amazing speed and dexterity. The boat eased to a slow drift, and Seh looked over at Fu.

Fu's eyes were fixed on a point in the distant darkness, and a group of soldiers soon came into view. They were standing before a set of the largest doors Seh had ever seen. Several of the horsemen began to point toward the boat, and two of them spurred their horses, charging toward Charles' sloop.

Fu fired.

The cannon erupted with a thunderous *BOOM!*, and smoke filled the air around Fu. Fortunately, there was a bit of a breeze blowing across the deck, and the air cleared almost immediately. Seh saw Fu place the burning slow match between his teeth and begin to reload the cannon.

Seh looked toward the soldiers and saw that Fu's shot had knocked one of the advancing men off his horse. That soldier would not be rejoining the fight.

The remaining charging horseman continued to race toward their boat, and Seh said, "I've got him."

"No," Hok said. "Save your cannons for multiple attackers. He's mine."

As the horseman neared, he withdrew a pistol from the folds of his robe and aimed it wildly at the boat. Hok did not let him get off the shot. Seh heard the *crack!* of the musket the same instant he saw the soldier tumble from his horse, a neat hole between his eyes.

"Wow," Charles said. "Remind me to never make *you* angry."

"You taught me well," Hok replied.

"Uh-oh!" Malao cried, and Seh looked over to see half of the horsemen spur their horses to life. At least thirty-five soldiers charged toward the boat.

"Here we go!" Charles shouted. "There is no turning back now. I am going to run us aground to give us a more stable platform to shoot from. Wait for my signal, then make every shot count!"

Charles steered the boat toward the shore and let

go of the helm. He picked up one of the many loaded muskets he kept handy and put it to his shoulder.

Seh heard a scraping noise, and the bow of the boat rushed up onto the soft muck of the shoreline. When the boat finally stopped rocking, the soldiers were almost within pistol shot.

"Fire!" Charles yelled.

Fu fired first. His cannon blast sent a horseman flying, and before the man hit the ground, Seh had fired off a shot, as had Hok, Charles, and Malao.

Soldiers began to shout, and Fu roared back in anger as Seh took aim and fired his second cannon. He had loaded this one with grapeshot—hundreds of lead balls the size of grapes. He could not believe the damage caused as it took down several soldiers.

Hok, Malao, and Charles continued to shoot as a few horsemen returned fire, then Charles bellowed, "Cease fire!"

The smoke cleared, and Seh saw that between the five of them, they had obliterated the attacking horsemen in what seemed like the blink of an eye. Every soldier was down. Who needed kung fu when you had weapons like these?

"Here come some more!" Malao called out from the mast top, and Seh saw another group of horsemen advancing toward them. The remaining pack had split, and nearly twenty soldiers were barreling toward them with pistols drawn. Seh and Fu scrambled to reload their cannons.

The next wave of soldiers came, but they did not

venture within range of Seh's grapeshot-filled cannon, so he did not fire. He saw with dismay that they were not able to do anywhere near as much damage without his deadly but short-range grapeshot. They managed to take down ten or eleven soldiers, but the rest remained unscathed, firing their pistols. The soldiers' shots ricocheted around the boat, but fortunately neither Seh nor the others seemed to get hit.

The soldiers retreated once their pistols had been spent, and they regrouped, huddling atop their horses in a circle beyond the range of firearms. Seh noticed that all of them had short bows and quivers of arrows strapped to the sides of their saddles.

"Is everyone okay?" Charles asked as the smoke cleared.

Amazingly, everyone replied that they were fine.

Seh's ears were ringing from all the noise, but even so he thought he heard a rushing noise, like the sound of running water. He turned toward the center of the deck, expecting to see a leak. Instead, he saw black powder pouring out of several holes in the oak barrels. Neither he nor any of the others had been hit because not all of the soldiers had been aiming at them. Some had been aiming at the stack of barrels, which were clearly labeled with large Chinese characters: Black Powder!

"Charles, look!" Seh cried, pointing at the powder accumulating on deck.

"Huh?" Charles replied. "Oh, no!"

The horsemen broke their circle and formed a line,

and Seh saw that each man held his short bow and three flaming arrows.

"What do we do?" Seh asked Charles. "Dump the powder overboard?"

"Too late," Charles said.

The horsemen began to charge, and Charles yelled, "Abandon ship!"

"Never!" Fu roared.

Hok grabbed Fu's wrist and yanked him toward the stern of the boat, which was nearest the deepest water. Seh watched her dive in, followed by huge splashes from Charles and Fu. Seh heard a long, shrill screech followed by a small splash, as Malao leaped from somewhere high atop the rigging.

Two flaming arrows passed over Seh's head, and he fired his cannons in a final act of defiance.

BOOM!

BOOM!

Several soldiers were torn from their horses, and Seh dove into the canal's icy water. The shock took his breath away, yet he still kicked and swam underwater with all his might until he thought his lungs would burst.

Then Charles' boat exploded.

The massive shock wave blasted Seh clear out of the water, and he managed to gulp in two mouthfuls of air before splashing back down. Pieces of charred wood and twisted iron began to fall from the sky, and he dove once more beneath the surface, staying down as long as he could. Something heavy bumped against his arm as it sank, and he pushed it away, remembering the time his mother had nearly drowned him. He hated swimming.

When Seh surfaced again, he found things eerily still. No more debris fell, and the canal water rocked gently from the aftermath of the blast. His ears were ringing even more now, and he was winded from holding his breath so long. Other than that, he seemed fine. He spotted the burning hulk of what remained of Charles' boat, and tried to decide which way to swim. The shore opposite the soldiers seemed like the obvious choice, but then a noise made him look toward the Forbidden City's main gate. He could hardly believe his eyes and ears. The bandits had arrived!

Mong, Hung, Sanfu, NgGung, and Bing were atop horses, accompanied by a thin old man who Seh had never seen before. They were literally riding circles around the remaining soldiers. While the soldiers rode fine horses, the bandits and the old man were on even more beautifully proportioned, muscular animals, with coats that practically shimmered in the moonlight. The bandits shot several of the soldiers, and as Seh began to swim toward that shore, he saw the old man pull a long rope from a bag tied to his saddle.

Still riding in a circle around the soldiers, the old man threw the rope over one of Tonglong's men and yanked him to the ground. The old man let go of the rope, and Sanfu leaped from his horse. He ran over to the man and tied him up.

The old man produced a second rope and began to

swing it in a wide loop over his head. By the time Seh reached shore, that rope was around another dismounted soldier and Bing was beside the soldier, tying him up like a butcher might bind a pig.

As the old man pulled a third rope from the bag, Seh saw a mob of men rush through the darkness on foot toward the bandits and Tonglong's horsemen. Fortunately, he recognized most of these newcomers, having trained them at the bandits' camp. They were on the bandits' side. They used their spears and swords admirably, dispatching any soldier who did not willingly surrender.

Seh pulled himself onto the bank and lay there, exhausted. He glanced around, looking for the others, and saw them all together down the shoreline. He waved, and they waved back.

Seh smiled with relief. They appeared to be fine. He looked back toward the bandits and saw NgGung approaching atop a spectacular horse. Seh thought he felt the ground begin to vibrate, and he compared what he felt with the rhythm of the horse's hooves. They did not match.

NgGung jumped out of his saddle and hurried over to Seh. The horse had stopped, but the vibrations continued.

"Are you okay?" NgGung asked.

"I thought so," Seh replied. "But now I'm not so sure. Feel the ground. Am I imagining things?"

NgGung knelt and rested his hand on the soft shore. His brow furrowed, and he ran several paces away from the water to firmer, drier ground, placing his ear against the earth.

"What is it?" Seh asked. "An earthquake?"

NgGung lifted his head, and Seh saw that his face had turned deathly pale in the moonlight.

"No. It's an army."

CHAPTER 26

Long stood inside the Emperor's suite, peering out one of the windows into the moonlit surroundings. The Emperor's palace was one of the tallest structures within the Forbidden City, and the suite was situated at the very top of the palace. It afforded a clear view of most of the complex.

Next to Long, Xie stared out of a second window. Across the room, Ying stared out of a third. As Wuya had said, there were soldiers positioned everywhere, including on the roof looking down over the windows. Long could see their shadows in the moonlight.

Long felt betrayed by Wuya. He could not even imagine how Xie must feel.

Together, Long and Xie watched Wuya and Tonglong

advance through gate after gate on their way toward the Emperor's palace. With them were four of Tonglong's soldiers in red, each carrying one corner of a large crate. Long remembered aloud Hok saying that she'd seen the Emperor being loaded into a crate, and Ying added that ShaoShu had told him a similar story. Long could not imagine anyone being caged in that, *especially* the Emperor.

Outside the Forbidden City, there was activity, too. All three of them had seen something that looked like fireflies next to the canal in the distance; muzzle flashes from muskets or pistols. They also saw bursts of flame from cannons, and heard their distinctive *booms.*

It seemed likely that Tonglong's men were engaging one of their enemies, but Long did not know which one. He assumed it was the bandits, because it was a smaller-scale attack, and he hoped to learn more if Wuya and Tonglong came to them. Wuya had communicated with many different soldiers as they walked, and he was sure to know what was going on. Whatever it was was obviously of little concern to Wuya or Tonglong in the safety of the Forbidden City, for both of them continued their march in the direction of the palace.

Suddenly there was an enormous explosion at the battle scene. A huge ball of fire rose into the sky, and Tonglong and Wuya turned to watch it for a moment. In the moonlight, Long could see that Tonglong was laughing heartily. Wuya did not appear to react in any manner. He just turned back toward the palace and continued walking.

"Xie," Long said. "What do you think Wuya and Tonglong are up to?"

"It seems obvious that Wuya has sold himself and his loyalty to Tonglong," Xie replied.

"Yes," Long said, "but why keep the Emperor alive? How come Tonglong does not just seize the throne?"

"He might have been able to do that with his army and an outright assault on the Forbidden City, but in a political takeover such as Tonglong is attempting there must be substantial documentation. I suspect they are keeping the Emperor alive because Tonglong needs the imperial seals. The Emperor keeps them hidden, and only he knows the hiding place."

"Couldn't Tonglong just make new seals?" Ying asked.

"He could, but it would require finding a master seal maker and then waiting months for all of them to be duplicated from previously sealed documents. Tonglong does not appear to be a very patient man."

"You have no idea how impatient and obsessive he can be," Ying said. "Xie, you are the Emperor's personal bodyguard. Where do you think he keeps his seals?"

"My best guess would be somewhere in this room."

"What?" Ying said, stepping away from the window. "That means Tonglong and Wuya are probably coming here right now! We need to get ready."

"There is nothing to get ready for," Xie said. "We will have to take things as they come. If the opportunity to fight presents itself, we shall. However, this is highly unlikely. There are three thousand Forbidden City soldiers out there, and they all report to Wuya. We can't fight that. Besides, Wuya will never present himself as a target. He carries two pistols that hold two shots each. They are of the finest quality, and he is the best shot in China. How do you think he came to be the head of security?"

"I will take my chances," Ying said, glancing around. "I spent a little time in one of the Emperor's prisons. I will never go back. Death is preferable." His eyes locked on the main suite door, and he hurried over to it, then ran his fingers along the wall around it. Here, the wall was made up of small decorative bricks. Ying removed his boots, and Long saw that his toenails were extraordinarily long, just like the nails on his fingers.

Ying jammed his toes and fingers into spaces between the wall bricks, and he began to climb. He positioned himself over the doorway, holding fast like an eagle clinging to the side of its nest.

Long looked back out of the window and saw that Wuya and Tonglong had disappeared. A few moments later, Long heard talking on the other side of the door. People were coming. He heard Wuya say, "We are about to enter the Emperor's private suite. I believe the seals are hidden here. Inside you will also find the surprises I mentioned earlier. Brace yourself."

Someone placed a key within the lock, and Long backed away from the door. It opened, and Wuya entered with Tonglong and the four soldiers carrying the large dilapidated crate. The crate reeked of neglected pigs. In the hall stood several Forbidden City soldiers, standing guard.

Tonglong saw Long and Xie, and he laughed. "Unbelievable! The two most wanted individuals on my criminal list, and here they are, waiting for me inside my new chambers. Wuya, perhaps I will let you be the one to execute Xie. It would be fitting for you to take his title as the new Western Warlord by removing his head with a jade sword. The stone is surprisingly sharp."

"You will pay for this, Wuya!" Xie said. "If not in this lifetime, in the next."

Wuya shrugged and stepped backward into the doorway.

Long saw movement out of the corner of his eye, and he noticed that Tonglong was adjusting his long, thick ponytail braid over the shoulder of his white jade armor.

Ying must have noticed, too, because while Tonglong was preoccupied, he struck. Ying released his grip on the wall and soared through the air toward Tonglong with his arms held up and back in a classic eagle-style kung fu pose. However, Tonglong happened to look up at that same instant, and he ducked.

Ying missed Tonglong and landed with a thud atop one side of the wooden crate. The jarring force of his heavy landing caused the four soldiers to lose their grip, and the crate crashed onto the suite's hard wooden floor, splintering into a hundred pieces. A foul stench filled the room.

Ying rolled away, shaking his head as if he were dazed, and Long saw a man lying inside the remains of the opposite side of the crate from where Ying had crashed. The man was seemingly half-dead. His face was sallow and covered in a woolly matted beard, and his clothes were little more than deeply stained shreds. He spied Xie and struggled to sit up.

"Emperor!" Xie shouted. He bolted for the ragged man, and two of Tonglong's soldiers sprang into action. They lunged at Xie, one low and one high.

Xie leaped cleanly over the lower man, but the soldier who went high struck Xie square in the sternum with his shoulder. The collision ended in a stalemate, with both men dropping to their knees. The soldier held a pistol in one hand, and he slammed the butt of it into the side of Xie's head. The impact caused the pistol to fire, the recoil driving the pistol butt against Xie's skull a second time.

Xie dropped into unconsciousness.

Long could see the other soldier raising his pistol toward Xie when the soldier was shot himself. An instant later, the man who'd knocked Xie out was shot dead, as were Tonglong's two remaining soldiers. Long looked into the doorway and saw Wuya holding two large pistols. Both pistol barrels were smoking. Wuya winked at Long.

Tonglong roared and pointed at Wuya. "You have made me play the fool! Your game all along has been to get the Emperor back here alive, hasn't it?"

Wuya smirked.

Tonglong howled. He raised the white jade sword and leaped at the Emperor.

Long leaped, too. Closer to the Emperor than Tonglong, he got there first and yanked the ragged ruler to the ground. Tonglong tried to spin and adjust his swing downward, but could not compensate enough. The sword missed by a handbreadth. Tonglong snapped his head around, and at the same time Long saw Ying rip Grandmaster's sword from his sash and dive recklessly toward them.

From the corner of his eye, Long noticed the end of Tonglong's ponytail braid swinging toward the Emperor. Ying reached out and grabbed its knotted end, then cried out. He slashed at the braid with Grandmaster's sword, severing it close to Tonglong's head. Tonglong's remaining hair spilled out like black water.

Ying cursed, and Long saw that he was still holding the end of the braid. It was stuck to his hand with a series of metal barbs that had been hidden within the knot of hair. Ying tugged at the tangled mass and ripped it from his palm. He hurled it across the room, tottered, and then fell.

Tonglong erupted with laughter. "A little trick from my dear mother, AnGangseh. Those barbs are tipped with her favorite poison."

Ying struggled to stand, and Long rushed to his side. "What are you doing?" Long whispered. "Stop moving. Slow your heart rate. I will find you an antidote."

Ying shook his head. "There is no antidote for what

I have done. Finish my fight, Long. China is counting on you." He pressed the sword into Long's left hand and slipped his extra-long chain whip out of its sleeve pocket, into Long's right hand. "*Eagle Returns Home—* do you remember it?"

"The chain whip maneuver? Yes."

"Attack Tonglong's left side with it. Use our grand-father's sword to distract his right."

Long felt his heart warm, glad that Ying knew of their connection.

Ying sat up suddenly and shoved Long aside with surprising force. He stood and half-stumbled, half-lunged at Tonglong.

"No!" cried Long, snatching at Ying's robe, but he missed.

Ying threw himself at Tonglong, swiping at Tong-long's face with a perfectly formed eagle-claw fist tipped with five razor-sharp fingernails. Surprised, Tonglong reacted with a simple parry, thrusting the white jade sword in his hand at Ying's stomach. Ying could easily have stepped to one side, but he did not. Instead, he allowed the jade blade to slide deep into his abdomen as he followed through with his blow.

Long saw Ying's fingernails dig deep into Tong-long's left eye. Tonglong screamed and backed away, and Ying slumped to the ground in a bloody heap, the white jade sword wedged inside him.

Long hissed like a dragon and headed for Tong-long.

Tonglong squinted at Long with his remaining

good eye and reached down for the jade sword's hilt protruding from Ying's torso. He was too slow.

Long raised Grandmaster's sword in his left hand and snapped his right arm forward with all his might, unfurling the chain whip and sending its sharp weighted tip at Tonglong's left side.

Tonglong dodged to his right, avoiding the end of the chain whip, and Long thrust Grandmaster's sword to Tonglong's right. Tonglong swung his head back to the left to avoid the sword, and Long snapped his right arm back, yanking the chain whip's weighted tip back toward himself.

The combination Ying had suggested worked perfectly. The sharp weight at the end of the chain whip continued its path back toward Long—the eagle flying back home—and buried itself into the back of Tonglong's head on his sightless left side.

Tonglong dropped like a stone, never to rise again.

CHAPTER 27

Long let his weapons fall to the floor and hurried over to Ying's side. Ying was barely breathing. There was blood everywhere. Long reached out, tracing his finger along the grooves in Ying's carved face.

Ying opened his eyes. "Is it done?" he asked, his voice little more than a whisper.

"Yes," Long replied. "You did it."

Ying shook his head slowly. "*We* did it, cousin." He shifted his gaze toward the Emperor, who was still on the floor nearby. They locked eyes, and Ying smiled.

"What is it?" the Emperor asked.

"You are a changed man," Ying said. "I can tell, for I have changed as well. It feels good, doesn't it?"

The Emperor nodded. "It certainly does, young eagle."

"His name is Saulong—Vengeful Dragon," Long said. "Is it not?"

"It is indeed," Ying replied, still smiling.

The Emperor bowed his head to Ying. "I offer you my deepest gratitude, young dragon. I have been humbled by this whole experience, but most of all by your selfless actions. Your name will not be forgotten."

"That is all anyone can ever hope for," Ying said, his smile somehow growing stronger still, and he closed his eyes.

Long grabbed Ying's hand and felt a surge of energy in his *dan tien* as Ying's spirit left him. Long lowered his head as Ying's hand grew cool in his own.

"It seems I also owe you my deepest gratitude," the Emperor said to Long.

"I did what needed to be done," Long replied. "I am glad that it is over."

Wuya entered from the doorway and placed his arm around the Emperor, helping him stand. "Let us hope this is the end of it," Wuya said. "We need to find out what has happened outside the gates."

Xie moaned, and Long looked over to see him stagger to his feet, rubbing his head.

"You are alive!" Wuya said. "Sometimes it is a blessing to have a hard head, old friend."

Xie looked at the holes in Tonglong's soldiers, and he turned to Wuya. "Did you do that?"

Wuya nodded. "I apologize for misleading you, but the Emperor's safety is my sworn priority. I needed to do everything within my power to isolate him and keep him alive, and I was unsure whom I could trust. I would put my life in your hands, of course, but Long—he is from Cangzhen Temple. You know the rocky history between their Grandmaster and the Emperor. After what I just witnessed, however, it is evident whose side Long is on."

Xie nodded.

Long was about to speak when he thought he heard someone sobbing softly. He looked toward the secret passageway and saw ShaoShu just inside its doorway. The small boy was soaking wet.

"Little Mouse!" Long said, rushing over to him. "What are you doing here?"

ShaoShu sniffled, his chest heaving. "I—I came to tell Ying that Tonglong was here. They are both dead, aren't they?"

Long put his hands on ShaoShu's shoulders. "I am afraid so."

The tears began to fall faster from ShaoShu's eyes. "Ying and Hok were the first friends I ever had. I am going to miss him."

"Me too," Long said. "Me too."

The Emperor came over, leaning on Wuya. "Hello, ShaoShu," he said. "Do you know who I am?"

ShaoShu nodded. "You're the Emperor."

"That's right," the Emperor replied. "I want to thank you for everything you did for me while I was held prisoner."

ShaoShu wiped his eyes and shrugged. "You're welcome."

"I just heard you say that you came here with Ying. Do you have someplace to go from here?"

ShaoShu shook his head.

"Why don't you stay here?" the Emperor said. "The Forbidden City can be a fun place for a boy."

ShaoShu's eyes widened and he wiped his nose on his sleeve. "Really?"

"Really."

Wuya knelt and handed ShaoShu a handkerchief from his sash. "Hello, Little Mouse. My name is Wuya, and I am the head of security here at the Forbidden City. My position does not allow me to marry, but I have always wanted a son. You could stay at my house. I live right across the courtyard from the Emperor. I even have an extra bedroom."

Long saw ShaoShu's eyes brighten. "I've never had my own room before," ShaoShu said.

Wuya stood. "Then it's settled."

"You will like it here, ShaoShu," Xie said from across the room. "Trust me. Now—"

Xie froze, and Long saw that he was looking out a window. "I don't believe it!" Xie said.

Long ran to the window and looked into the gray dawn. There were large fires burning along the walls of the Forbidden City. "Signal fires?" he asked.

"Yes," Xie replied. "My troops have arrived. Or some of them, anyway. My easternmost mounted armies could have made it here by now. We should feel the pounding of their horses' hooves soon. If we were at ground level, we would already feel it."

"Will they be enough to defeat Tonglong's army?" Long asked. "I mean, his huge force working its way in our direction."

"I do not believe we need to fear Tonglong's army anymore," Xie said. "What do you think, Wuya?"

Wuya shook his head. "From what I learned communicating with Tonglong's men, he had no second in command, which makes sense if you consider how he was Ying's second in command and went on to double-cross Ying. Tonglong would probably never trust any one person as his second, so he likely had many people performing small pieces of that role."

"What about Commander Woo?" Long asked.

Wuya shook his head. "I was told that Commander Woo once broke his own leg while attempting to duplicate a kick he saw in a dragon scroll. He is no threat. I have been told that he is only capable of following orders, at best."

"What about the Eastern Warlord?" Long asked. "Is he not still leading Tonglong's main army?"

The Emperor laughed. "The Eastern Warlord is only interested in living a life of luxury. He has no interest in conquest. Tonglong forced him at gunpoint to join the coup attempt. He will always take the easy road, and that will be the road I lay out for him. He will comply."

"What will happen to Tonglong's army?" Long asked.

"I will begin the process of dissolving it immediately," the Emperor said, taking charge. "I am certain the majority of the new recruits will be on their way home by the end of the week. Right now, however, we need to get the whole story."

The Emperor turned to Wuya. "Go and collect as much information as possible. Meet me in the banquet hall for a full briefing in three hours. Bring any advisors you deem necessary, and take ShaoShu with you. He has likely gleaned useful information from his time with Tonglong, and should be quite helpful. Besides, he is now under your wing."

"Yes, Sire!" Wuya bowed.

"Xie," the Emperor said. "I need protection until we know the full nature of our situation. I know that you are the Western Warlord, but for now, will you serve as my personal bodyguard?"

Xie bowed. "Of course, Sire."

The Emperor looked at Long. "It would please me if you were to join us for the briefing as well. Until then, I promise we will attend to your cousin's remains. Wuya can escort you to the banquet hall on his way out. If you should require anything, just ask the soldiers stationed outside the room."

"Thank you, Sire," Long replied with a bow.

"Well," the Emperor said, scratching his filthy beard, which still reeked from the pig crate. "Now that these things are in motion, it is time to take care of the most important items of all." He clapped his hands twice, and attendants hurried into the suite. "Draw me a bath," he commanded, "and tell the chefs to prepare a midmorning feast of all my favorite dishes. But no pork."

Three hours later, Long sat alone at a huge rectangular table inside the Emperor's exquisite banquet hall. The sun had risen, and light reflected off a thousand gilded surfaces, casting strange shadows across the ornate floor. The shadows reminded Long of the dark pools of blood that had surrounded Ying. At least Ying had died happy.

Long supposed that he was happy, too, in a sense. His grandfather had asked him and his temple siblings to change the Emperor's heart, as well as Ying's. That much had been accomplished.

The banquet hall door opened, and Long looked up to see Xie enter alongside the Emperor. Like Long, Xie appeared weary and battle-worn, his skin and clothing a mess. The Emperor, on the other hand, looked like a new man. His face had been shaved, and someone had trimmed his hair. He now wore brilliant yellow robes, and despite his sallow cheeks and pale skin, he looked every bit the distinguished ruler that he was.

Long rose from his seat and bowed, and the Emperor crossed the room to sit in a throne at the head of the table. Xie sat at the Emperor's right. Long remained where he was, near the center of the table. He sat back down after a nod from Xie.

The Emperor clapped twice, and Wuya entered the doorway flanked by three Forbidden City soldiers. Each soldier carried a white jade sword, and all four men dropped to their knees, kowtowing.

"Rise," the Emperor said.

The men rose, and the three soldiers took positions beside the doorway.

Wuya addressed the Emperor. "In an effort to provide you with the fullest report possible, I have invited several 'advisors' to join us. I hope it is not too many, Sire."

"We shall see," the Emperor replied.

Wuya poked his head out through the doorway, and ShaoShu scurried in first. He bowed quickly and said, "Hi! I can't wait for you to meet my friends."

The Emperor chortled. "Of course, ShaoShu. Come in."

Fu, Malao, Seh, Hok, and Charles entered next as a group. Long smiled broadly.

"May I present three young men and one young

lady from Cangzhen Temple," Wuya said, "along with their Dutch friend, Charles. From left to right, the young monks are Fu, Malao, Seh, and Hok."

The group members bowed in unison, and the Emperor nodded to them. "Greetings, young ones. I have some things to say to you, but not just yet. Please, have a seat beside Long."

They sat down at the table on either side of Long.

Wuya turned to the door again, and Mong, Hung, Sanfu, NgGung, and Bing walked into the room. A stern-looking soldier in a brown and black silk uniform followed them. The group bowed as one.

"You may sit," the Emperor said, gesturing toward the magnificent empty chairs across the table from Long and the others.

The bandit group sat, and the Emperor looked at the soldier. "You are General Zo of Xie's army, are you not?"

The man jumped to his feet. "Yes, Sire."

"Give me your report."

"There is not much to report, Your Eminence. My Eastern legions and I were out on patrol when Xie ordered us here to deal with Tonglong and his conscripted army. You may have felt the earth tremble as we approached. There are ten thousand of us, and we all ride Heavenly Horses. We could easily turn away fifty thousand trained foot soldiers, let alone a new army such as Tonglong's."

"I am glad to have you on my side," the Emperor said. "How long can you and your men stay?"

"As long as you can feed us, Sire."

"Excellent. Please, sit."

The general sat down, and the Emperor looked at Mong. The bandit leader rose.

"Although we have not always been on the same side," the Emperor said, "I have a need for great men in my army. From what I have heard over the years, you are a great man. As you know, Tonglong had most recently been the Southern Warlord. Would you be willing to assume the role?"

Mong smiled. "Thank you, Your Eminence. I must say, that is the last thing I expected to hear. It would be an honor."

The Emperor nodded and turned to Wuya. "I see that you have found the white jade swords."

"Yes, Sire," Wuya replied, standing. "Two were found secured to the saddle of the horse Tonglong rode here. The third is the one Tonglong carried. The armor was rather in need of a thorough cleaning."

"Bring the swords to me."

"As you wish, Sire," Wuya said, and he gestured to the solders flanking the door. They approached the Emperor.

The Emperor rose and took one of the swords. He held it out toward Mong. "Take this as proof of your status as the new Southern Warlord, and of your commitment to me."

Mong approached the Emperor, bowed, and took the sword.

The Emperor held out a second sword toward Xie,

and Xie stood. "Take this, comrade, as proof of your status as the new Western Warlord, and of your commitment to me."

Xie bowed and accepted the sword.

"You may be seated," the Emperor said, and Mong and Xie sat down, as did Wuya. The three soldiers returned to flank the door.

The Emperor gripped the third white jade sword and held it high. Long could tell by the jade's pattern that this was the sword that Tonglong had used against Ying.

"I am the Northern Warlord," the Emperor announced. "I will wear this sword as a symbol of that role. This is also the sword that took the life of a brave young man called Saulong, better known to many of you as Ying. Let it be a constant reminder to all of the ultimate sacrifice he made saving my life."

A few of the bandits cheered, and the Emperor continued, lowering the ceremonial weapon. "There are actually four white jade swords. I saw Tonglong with them inside the bowels of the Shanghai Fight Club. Do any of you know what has become of the remaining one? I believe Tonglong may have given it to the Eastern Warlord."

"I think he did, too," ShaoShu said. "I saw the Eastern Warlord carrying one around when I was in Shanghai."

"Very well," the Emperor said. "I will have this verified. It makes sense for him to have one. Now"—he turned to Long and the other Cangzhen warrior monks—"months ago, most of the kung fu temples in our great nation were destroyed as a result of the paranoia that was put in my mind by Tonglong and the deceased General Tsung—the Leopard Monk. They convinced me that these powerful centers of warrior prowess were a threat to me, and I approved their destruction. Now I find I owe my life to a group of very special young warrior monks. I want to honor them for what they have done for me personally and, more importantly, what they have done for all of China."

The Emperor paused and looked at the young heroes before him. "Fu, Malao, Seh, Hok, and Long—because of the contributions you have made to China's history, and because of the contributions I expect you will make in the future, I hereby dub you the Five Ancestors. Your names will become legend. Rise."

All five rose and bowed. Despite himself, Long felt his face flush with pride. He glanced at the others, and saw the same dazed glow about their faces.

"Likewise," the Emperor said, "the name of your temple brother, Ying, shall live on. Long live the memory of Saulong—the Vengeful Dragon!" Again he raised his white jade sword high, and the room erupted with cheers.

The table quieted, and the Emperor said, "So tell me, young warrior monks, what do you plan to do next? Let us start with you, Fu."

Fu shrugged and looked at Sanfu. "I don't know, sir, but whatever it is, I will be doing it with my father."

Sanfu beamed.

"Very good," the Emperor said. "What about you, Seh?"

"My answer is much the same as Fu's," Seh replied. "I will follow my father, Mong. I suppose we are moving to Hangzhou because of his new title. I look forward to it. I have never been there."

Mong nodded his appreciation to Seh, and the Emperor turned to Hok, gesturing for her to speak.

Hok looked at her mother. "I will remain with my mother, Bing. She and I have already discussed what we hope to do next, and that is to reunite with my father, Henrik, a Dutch sea captain. My sister, GongJee, will accompany us."

"Hey, can I go with you, too?" Malao asked. "I *love* boats!"

Hok looked at Bing, and Bing smiled. "If you wish, Malao. I believe Charles might be in search of a first mate, once we get him a new boat."

"Oh!" Malao said, turning to Charles. "Do you think I would be good enough?"

Charles laughed. "You have potential."

Malao clapped excitedly.

The Emperor turned to Long. "What about you, young dragon?"

Long knew exactly what he planned to do next, but he was not interested in sharing it with anyone. "I do not know," he replied.

The Emperor's smile widened. "I have an offer for you. When things have stabilized, Xie will be leaving for Tunhuang. I will be in need of a new personal bodyguard. As this year's Fight Club Grand Champion, you would be a perfect choice. Not to mention the fact that your dedication and loyalty are unquestionable."

"Thank you for the generous offer, Your Eminence," Long said, "but I am afraid I will have to decline."

The Emperor appeared taken aback. "What? It takes a brave man to refuse the Emperor, you know."

Long did not wish to offend him. He decided it was better to answer the question. "I plan to go to Cangzhen Temple."

"Really?" ShaoShu interjected. "I was just there. There is hardly anything left. Everything has been burned."

"Exactly," Long replied. "I will rebuild it."

There was a pleased murmur along the length of the table, and Wuya said, "Pardon me, Sire, but Tonglong stole a fortune from Ying's—I mean Saulong's—family. He gave much of that treasure to me, believing he was buying my support. Since Saulong and Long are cousins, that treasure is rightfully Long's."

Long shook his head. "Saulong's mother, my aunt, is still very much alive. The treasure belongs to her."

The Emperor rubbed his freshly shaven chin. "You will need to fund the rebuilding somehow, Long. Let me help. I owe you at least that much."

Long paused. He remembered the trouble his grandfather had gotten into taking money from the Emperor. On the other hand, he would likely never be able to raise enough on his own, and he possessed none. "Thank you for the generous offer," he said. "May I think about it? Oftentimes, we dragons like to do things our own way, even if it makes life more difficult."

"Of course," the Emperor said. "Take all the time you need. Now, who is ready for a celebration?"

The Emperor clapped his hands twice, and servants began to pour into the banquet hall, carrying tray after tray of elaborately prepared food. Malao and Fu looked at each other with huge smiles, and Shao-Shu squealed with delight.

"I hope they aren't serving Greasy Goose!" Malao said.

Fu blushed, and Sanfu laughed. "I see it affects you the same way it affects me, son. Nothing to be ashamed of. If Malao gives you any more trouble, let me know and we'll sit on either side of him with Greasy Goose drumsticks in our hands. His stinky feet kung fu will have nothing on us."

The bandits and the young monks all broke into laughter and began to talk among themselves. Everyone, that is, except Long. He stood, suddenly feeling as though the walls were closing in around him. He bowed to the Emperor and approached the throne. "Pardon me, Sire, but I could use a little fresh air."

"Certainly," the Emperor said. "Wuya can show you the way to the courtyard. It is a fine winter day."

"If it is all the same to you, Your Eminence, I would prefer to show myself out."

"As you wish."

Long bowed again and slipped out of the room. Instead of heading for the courtyard, however, he went directly to the Emperor's suite. No one stopped him.

Long blinked as he entered alone the room where just three hours ago his life had changed forever. Ying's and Tonglong's remains had been taken away, and the floors had already been scrubbed clean. All that remained were a few small puddles that would soon dry and disappear. It was almost as if nothing had occurred here.

Almost.

In the back corner of the room, Long saw Ying's chain whip and their grandfather's sword resting on an ornate table. He walked over and picked up the items. He was not sure how he felt about someone separating these things from Ying's body, but at least the weapons had been treated with the utmost respect. Both had been thoroughly cleaned and dried, and someone had even coated the sword's blade with a thin sheen of oil to help protect it against rust. Long nodded his approval.

He unfurled the chain whip and wrapped it around his waist like a sash, loosely tying the ends in front of him. This was how his grandfather used to carry his chain whip into battle.

Straight sword in hand, Long crossed the room and found the secret panel door that led to the Emperor's escape passageway. He had no key, but found that one was not necessary from this side. He opened the door, passed through it, and closed it tightly behind him. The others would understand if he did not say goodbye. They knew where they could find him.

Turning his back on the Forbidden City, Long headed for the ashes of Cangzhen Temple.

Like his main characters, **Jeff Stone** was an orphan who went in search of—and found—his birth parents. He also has a black belt in Shaolin-Do kung fu, which he tested for at the legendary Shaolin Temple in China. Originally from Detroit, Jeff lives in the Midwest with his wife and two children and their two dogs—sibling "schnoodles" Ricky and Roxie. Thanks to this series, he's also kept a number of snakes, mice, mountain horned dragons, scorpions, and praying mantids. To his wife's relief, all tiger, monkey, and crane research was done at the zoo.